YOURS LEGALLY

A collection of short stories…

Sonia Sahijwani

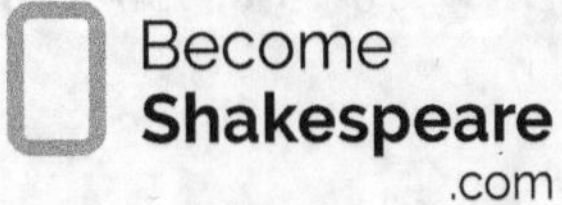

Published in 2019

Becomeshakspeare.com

Wordit Content Design & Editing Services Pvt Ltd
Unit - 26, Building A -1, Nr Wadala RTO,
Wadala (East), Mumbai 400037, India
T: +91 8080226699
Wordit Art Fund helps deserving authors publish their work by providing monetary support. To apply for funding, please visit us at www.BecomeShakespeare.com

ISBN - 978-93-88930-03-1

This one is definitely for you "Suhaan"….

ABOUT THE AUTHOR

Sonia Sahijwani is a 33 year old LL.B. graduate from Faculty of Law, Delhi University. After completing her graduation in Commerce from Delhi University (Gargi College), she pursued her Masters in Print Journalism (English) from Indian Institute of Mass Communication (IIMC), New Delhi. Pursuant to a brief stint with a leading financial magazine, she left her job to study law. She is currently working in a public sector company as a legal officer and is posted at Chandigarh alongwith her husband Sulabh Saini. She is presently enjoying motherhood and is busy parenting her six month old son Suhaan. This is her first book.

Know more about her at www.the-mind-and-heart-speaks. blogspot.com

Contact: sonyasahijwani@gmail.com

Disclaimer

This book is a work of fiction and any resemblance to any living character, place, event or incident (unless stated to the contrary by the author herein) is completely coincidental and unintentional. Names, characters and events have been used in a fictitious manner. The author has utmost respect for the field of law, for the country's legal and justice system and for the lawyers, the judges and the litigants. The stories have only been inspired from real life incidents and are not aimed at portraying any sort of adverse image of anyone.

But, to err is human. To add to it, to forgive is humane.

If at any point, I hurt any sentiments, I duly apologise for the same.

'Res ipsa loquitor'

(The thing speaks for itself)

Preface

The story behind this book:

I strongly believe God has put a little something extra while designing each one of us. We all have a passion, a hobby which is close to our heart and soul and which we secretly desire we could pursue professionally. It could be a sport, an interest in fine arts, music, photography or filmography, or something as rare as becoming a trekker or a wildlife adventurist. But it is inherently present in all of us.

Some recognize it at an early age, some others develop it over a period of time. And then there are the unfortunate ones who never get the opportunity to discover it within themselves. There are those lucky few (*particularly in our country where the focus remains on acquiring degrees*) who are able to make a career out of their hobby. As they say, make your hobby your work and you are going to enjoy each day of your work life. Sounds simple enough right? But we all know how tough it is given the struggle it entails and the financial risks involved. Unfortunately, our Indian parents still find solace in the fact that their child is employed in a 9-5 secure stable job, earns a fixed salary per month and in case it is a Government job, then they are rest assured their child's future is in safe hands.

However, I truly believe that there is a unique sense of satisfaction one gets when one is doing something he/she loves and is passionate about. Hard work follows easily if one is truly in love with what one is doing. Talk about watching your favourite sport or movie, we all are willing to stay up late in the night. But talk about finishing off that boring presentation for upcoming client visit, we prefer to hit the sack instead and procrastinate it until the end.

Now why am I sounding so philosophical? The reason of stating all of the above is that I have been no different.

As far as my memory takes me back to my childhood, all I can remember is my intense love for writing. The idea of writing a book, my book, is a seed I was nurturing ever since I was a fifth standard student. Though I was extremely fond of academics, yet it was writing which brought me immense happiness and fulfillment which infact could not be expressed in words.

I still remember the first time, my first articles, two hindi poems, *"Fir Aya Basant"* and *"Pareeksha ke ek din pehle"* which featured in the same annual edition of our school magazine **"New Horizons"**. It elated me immensely. Seeing my name out there thrilled me, more than that, creating something using words and my imagination brought me utmost satisfaction.

As we went in senior classes, a popular female TV and film Actor and back in 1996 a famous theatre artist, who had joined my school for a brief stint who actually inculcated the habit of diary writing in us particularly in me. She told us each to have our own personal diary and write two to three pages every single day. It could be about our favourite TV show, the latest news headlines or simply our daily activities, but we had to give one hour each day for this particular activity and read it out in the class the next day.

And I vividly remember, I was among the 2-3 students who were committed to this at the outset itself. It was perhaps this habit which became a part of me and I need to thank her now for something which she gave me perhaps 20 years ago.

I do not think anyone even knows this barring a few close ones but I was crazy about writing to the extent that I simply loved, and actually looked forward to writing exams. Sad! But it's the truth!

The one thing students dread and wish fervently they don't fail in, I have been obsessed about writing exams from school life itself. However, it was while pursuing Law that I reached the epitome of writing as this field involved well, a hell lot of writing. I still remember the look on my friend's faces when I would state that I love Jurisprudence (theories on law) and I enjoyed teaching them the subject as well.

The subjects my friends hated during law school specially drafting pleadings, interpretation of statutes and jurisprudence turned out to be my favourites as they gave me a lot of scope and room to experiment with the creative side of me. I feel all this and more played a critical role in augmenting the writer side of me. And that's all the more reason its significant here to thank one of my (*then*) good friend *Sid* who actually pushed me into pursuing law. Little did I know then that my stint with law school followed by working in the legal profession would be the perfect ingredients for my debut book. We may not be in touch now but if by any chance you are reading this, I owe you buddy.

It may infact sound bizarre but the first draft of this book was actually written way back in the year 2012, yes, six long years ago and believe me it's the hard truth. I had shared my manuscript with many publishing companies earlier only to receive rejections or no responses. And trust me, waiting for even a simple response be it a rejection, is the toughest thing to do for any budding author.

It's perhaps the same as auditioning for several roles and waiting for the right script to come your way. In this case, the script was ready but the producer and director were awaited. Receiving no response did crush my spirits for a long time and I put aside this draft to rework on it later. But it never dampened my spirit to write and I continued to hone it by maintaining my blog over the past few years. I thank *Pardeep and GK, my two close friends* for always pushing me and encouraging me to write and being my most loyal and critical readers.

Returning to the story behind this story, the first draft was written, sent to many publishers, and on receiving no response continued to stay in my PC and hard drive for well, a really long while. Meanwhile, life is what happens when you are busy making other plans and marriage, change of jobs, moving to another city and then having a kid made me fully occupied in the daily grind and routine like everyone else.

But deep inside, the desire to get my book published and see my name on the cover of my own creation was simply not leaving my thoughts. And it seems the wait of past six years finally paid off. Just while I was busy playing mommy to my five month old son, recently one fine afternoon, while I was checking my personal email, awaiting some documents from my hubby, an email got my particular attention.

It was a mail from a certain **Leadstart Publishing** which seemed completely out of the blue. Amidst the spam mails and endless promotional emails which kept filling my inbox each day, I read *"Legally Yours"* (*the then working title*) as the subject of the mail which surprised me in an eccentric way. With wide eyes, I opened the mail only to be shocked on reading that they had responded to the draft I had sent six years ago. To be very honest it took me a while to recall and realize what had I written so long back and how on earth was it being talked about now.

The contents of the mail brought a wide grin on my face as I was informed that I was now eligible for Wordit Art Fund, their sister concern which is assisting budding writers in getting their books published without going through the cumbersome process of traditional booksellers and without the authors having to make a hefty investment. The fact that they were giving such opportunities to new authors and I was one among them, my happiness knew no bounds.

As advised in the email therein, I approached Ms Pooja Dutt from Wordit Art Fund and the rest as they say is history….

Prologue

Something about this book:

I vividly remember, even when I was in school, I used to argue a hell lot with my parents on anything and everything possible under the sun, (*something which I still do*). My father used to tell me mockingly, ***"tujhe toh vakil banna chahiye, bas behes karti rehti hai" (you must become a lawyer, you are always arguing with us).*** I never thought it might actually become true some day! Till I had joined law, I had absolutely no idea whatsoever about how the legal profession works since no one in my family nor anyone I knew close had ever pursued this field.

Yet, the legal subjects I had studied during graduation had captivated me and I was keen on giving it a shot. One thing led to another and one fine day I saw myself entering my law college with no idea whatsoever on what the next three years held in store for me.

Many people, including my relatives, friends, colleagues used to always ask me the perennial 2 questions, *"Why would you get into law after journalism? What is the connection between the two??!*

I tried hard to explain to them how journalism shaped up, enhanced and widened the way we thought, wrote, interacted and communicated. And that all these things were much useful and pertinent being in the legal profession which was all about good drafting, being a good orator, and communicating well particularly in the Court. But I knew most of them never understood it and after a point, I simply stopped explaining.

And now that this book is out, the answer to the above questions is also quite clear. This seems to me ultimate reason why to everyone's surprise I made the transition from journalism to the field of law. It amuses me how infact pursuing this profession led me to pen down my first book and enable me to fulfill the dream of becoming an author which I saw as a young girl.

I have to divulge, this legal profession is one of the most interesting and challenging professions one can be in. Its capricious, involves minute, elongated and careful reading between the lines and words and I mean literally deciphering the intent behind that comma and the purpose behind that particular semi colon. For the ones into litigation, it also entails immersing their minds till wee hours of morning into books and more books for case research and analysis of various laws, lots and lots of running around from the court, office, chamber, court, back to office and finally, loads and tons of patience.

Life in the legal fraternity is a small world in itself. Only those who have the placidity, audacity and the zeal stick around and make a mark in the longer run. Entering this field of law is perhaps not such a tough task, but establishing yourself as a decent enough reputed lawyer amidst the hundreds of lawyers entering this profession each day is definitely an uphill task. And I realized this in only a few trips to the court and the memories it gave me.

What interested me and inspired me most amidst all this is the diverse and enriching and sometimes stressful experiences one has in the courts in this country. Everytime in the court when I had a dreadful day because of the judge not passing a favourable order, or because of the endless hours of waiting, or simply agitated at the eccentric, slow and sometimes rather unfair the system of justice worked, I would make up my mind that I would never ever step inside the court premises again.

(Un)fortunately, it was all in vain as the next day, I would see myself getting ready for the matter with the same enthusiasm despite knowing that this very day might also end up like the day before as well. As uncanny as it may sound, this legal field purely makes you addicted to it.

Everyone wants to stay away from the law and the courts. Isn't it true enough? Being in the profession myself

I pray each day that my loved ones should never need to have any sort of connection with legal proceedings as we all know, it truly is a cumbersome exhausting ordeal. However, despite the fears and doubts, the field of law is a roller coaster ride and I am pretty sure once someone enters this territory it is more often than not extremely difficult to leave it.

With the above backdrop, perhaps now you my reader will have a faint idea about this book. To give you a small glimpse of what's in store let me just say that the book has been narrated through the eyes and ears of my protagonist Sia, a budding lawyer who tried out every possible training opportunity she could lay her hands on before finalizing on where she wanted to be after she finished her graduation.

The stories are a by product of certain incidents during her diverse experiences in the legal system as each one of them affected her and impacted her in some way and taught her something about life as well. She sometimes did it for the sole purpose of beautification of her CV, but mostly she did it for the real and genuine motive of getting acquainted with the legal process, learning the nuances of litigation(court practice), the nitti gritties of the profession thereby enabling them to gather some experience beforehand itself.

Sia explored the opportunities that came her way for all of the reasons above. Little did she know that her experiences would teach her not just law but something more as well.

Now normally, a book which is a compilation of short stories has an independent story each. Rarely are those stories interrelated or interconnected. Infact, while writing this book, I realized that trying to keep a story short and crisp is extremely challenging as compared to penning a single long story. This book is a tad different, as all the six stories herein have one common protagonist *Sia,* and one common thread which binds them all i.e. *Law.*

Each story revolves around one of the 6 elements which I feel are critical to this profession, the elements being; *the Case, the Court (Judge), the Counsel, the Complainant, the Confinement and the Criminal* (defendant or accused).

While the first three stories are based on the elements of *The Complainant, The Court and The Case* and are court room dramas with a dash of satire, the fourth story is based on the element *"The Counsel"* and is dedicated to a lawyer whom I personally had the experience of working with.

The last two stories are based on the elements of *The Confinement and The Criminal* and are the protagonist's eccentric but memorable experiences of visiting an Indian Prison. It is for all those who have only imagined how a prison is, seen in movies or heard from friends and have never ever seen in reality. Inspired by true incidents, the names of the prison and the accused have been withheld for obvious reasons.

I wish this book reaches out to not just those who are a part of the legal profession, but also the youth in particular who are trying to get back to the habit of reading, be it the e-way.

Whether you know anything about law or not, I hope this interests you, inspires you to enter this profession and perhaps impacts you in some way.

******

The Complainant

"Aequitas legem sequitor"

"Equity follows the law"

1. 99 Vs निन्यानवे

It had been few months since Sia finished her graduation in LLB. Luckily, she had been able to grab an opportunity to work with a Senior Advocate who was specializing in property law matters. Though she was not so keen in this subject, but nevertheless, she was right then completely focused on enhancing her CV and working under a reputed Senior was always a big deal.

A month had passed since she had joined Mr Kabir Mehta, Sr Adv at his office in a posh locality in Central Delhi. While she was initially very excited for her new stint, it took her mere few days to fathom that interning with a Senior Adv definitely has its pros and cons.

To start with, her presence was hardly even noticed by Mr Kabir, and there were days where he would walk right past her in the office without even taking a second look at her. It was the same fate during the court hearings as well. She would stand beside him the entire time only to be eventually given a handful of files to carry with to another court. It did hit her ego several times but she remained passive. Perhaps her senior was genuinely too busy to notice her.

To make matters worse, since Senior Advocates were mainly engaged by parties at the stage of arguments, hence Sia was not able to be involved from the nascent stages of a legal case which bugged her. She was yet to learn the nuances of filing court cases, of witnessing court proceedings. This was not the ideal beginning for a career in the legal field and she had already started looking for alternatives, though ofcourse secretly.

"Patience Sia, Patience", she used to tell herself, thinking that even the most famous of advocates would have once carried files like her within these four walls.

And while she was counting days and mentally preparing herself as to how would she tell Mr Kabir that she wished to quit so soon, one fine day, on 24.10.2009 something unusual happened which made her remember this training forever.

It was a usual day after court hours. There was a meeting going on in the cabin of her senior since afternoon and a bunch of five heavy looking men wearing white kurtas who seemed his clients were pacing all around the office in a panic mode *(It was later that Sia got to know who the real client was which shall be revealed in due course)*. The next moment out of nowhere Sia was summoned into his cabin. She was startled. This was the first time she was being called inside and it was considerably the most awaited moment for her all this while.

"So he remembers me after all", sighed Sia with a faint smile of relief and picked up her diary and pen with a newfound enthusiasm to finally be a part of a real case meeting.

Once inside facing her senior, she chose to remain silent for two reasons: one, she was there for the first time and second, she had absolutely no idea, no clue whatsoever about the case at hand as she had not read the file as yet. She was petrified for not being aware lest she is asked something related to the issue and she was constantly biting her lip in this fear.

While Sia strained herself to try to gauge the matter at hand, all she understood was that this was a property dispute between members of a family itself. The plaintiff's *(the party who has filed the suit)* had approached her senior lawyer pleading him to make an appearance on the next date of hearing on their behalf in a certain district court on the outskirts of Delhi which fell under the jurisdiction of one of the prominent states in North India. From their voices, it seemed they were fearing losing the case for the other party having immense political influence enough to turn the case in their favour.

The matter was at the stage of cross-examination. For the non-legal pals, it is pertinent to tell in brief about the purpose of this proceeding. The stage of cross-examination comes after examination-in-chief, wherein the plaintiff's own lawyer examines his/her client/plaintiff. In cross examination, the counsel of the opposite party/defendant examines the plaintiff/complainant.

However, since Mr Kabir rarely appeared in a district court, they were leaving no stone unturned in trying to convince him to plead on their behalf. By then Sia had atleast figured out that the men were brothers of the lady who was the real client but was yet to know who the opposite party was and what was the reason of the dispute.

Just as she was immersed in her thoughts, she heard a familiar voice addressed to her for the first time,

"What was your name again young lady?"

Bit hesitant and surprised at the turn of events, she fumbled for the first time while saying "Sss Sia, Sir,Sia Sen"

"Have you ever visited any court proceeding outside Delhi?" Mr Kabir enquired

"Umm..No Sir", Sia was fearing what came ahead but decided it was better to be honest at this stage.

"Have you ever witnessed a cross examination or examination in chief?"

She repeated, *"No, not really Sir"* she admitted as if confessing to a crime.

*"Ok then, tomorrow meet us sharp at 8am at the front gate here and you shall accompany me to the Court. Don't be late."*Mr Kabir sounded firm.

The command given, he gave her one more look, rose up from his chair, shook hands with the men and followed them outside till the front gate.

Sia did not know whether to be happy or scared or both. She had not even spoken to her parents about it. A Court proceeding in a court outside the capital city, what would that be like? Can she say no? What if she would have said no? What if her parents don't let her go? What did the man in blue jacket say? Why did such a senior advocate accept this case of a lower court that too from people who did not seem to be so well off? Sia was flooded with questions she had no answers to. By then, there was no room for all these doubts as the decision had been made and she had no option but to relent.

24th October 2009:

District Courts,(somewhere in a city in North India)

The D-day arrived. Though it was Sia's first cross examination mainly to witness, but she felt a part of it already. It was an important milestone for her in her short spell in the legal profession. She reached the office gate at sharp 8 am only to see her boss already waiting for her in his silver Honda City reading the day's newspaper. For some unexpected reason, her parents had agreed with the idea of her going to a court outside the city perhaps since her boss was also accompanying her.

Amidst all the chaos yesterday, she had forgotten to even take a look at the case at hand and she had never felt so silly and blank in her life. The file was kept on the arm rest at the back seat of the car where they were now seated between Sia and Mr Kabir but she could not muster up the courage to pick it up and go through it in front of him.

Besides a few phone calls and a short halt for water, the entire ride had been a quiet one as expected. She also kept wondering throughout the silent car ride what made him accept this case and why did he cancel his important hearings in the Supreme Court fixed for the day for this particular case. Little did she know she was going to know the real reason soon.

10.10.am

District Court

They had finally reached the court premises. Their matter was fixed in Court No. 5.

While Sia was busy looking around the court she was visiting for the first time, she realized that her senior had walked ahead and she rushed up to reach her boss. They were now standing in front of the court where their matter was listed as Item No. 10. The Metropolitan Magistrate came sharp on time and by 10.25am the proceedings of the day had begun.

She followed her senior inside the court room and since the front row had only one vacant seat, she went ahead and occupied a seat in the last bench. The last bench had become her favourite spot by now as it gave her a 360 degree view of the entire court room. She could see everyone, every minute proceeding clearly. She noticed that the lawyers inside the room were a bit surprised to see Mr Kabir Mehta among them. Almost every one of them present in the room came to him shook his hand and asked the perennial question which was bothering her since yesterday, *"Sir, Why are you here?!"*

She also saw the man in the blue coat from yesterday's meeting sitting in the second row ahead of her. At that moment, her eyes did not fall on the person sitting next to him as she could not imagine in her wildest of dreams that she could be their client after all.

"Item No. 10"

The moment had finally arrived. The instant their case was called, they geared up as it was once again time to face the action. Her senior counsel alongwith the local advocate went ahead to face the Hon'ble Magistrate. While Sia also rose to join them, just then, her eyes fell on a certain someone and got wedged. She noticed something uncanny. She saw a very old, fragile lady probably in her 80s, wearing a white saree, hair tied in a bun, getting up from the second row. She was being escorted by a man who seemed familiar to her. He was the same man in the blue Nehru jacket!

Wait, why was he with this lady? Were they related? Was she their client? Was she the one? Sia was flooded with all this and more and was thoroughly perplexed and astounded.

The lady in the white saree was holding a stick in one

hand and was being supported by the man from her other arm as he accompanied her towards the Magistrate. Sia saw the lady's hands were shivering and trembling while walking upto the front.

Sia was in a state of shock. She could not ever imagine even getting her 60+ years old parents to face such an ordeal. *And here was an old lady of perhaps her grandmother's age, who was here for god knows what'*, Sia muttered to herself, feeling helpless.

By then she was almost sure from what she witnessed that she was their client after all. She also realized why the old lady would have been unable to attend the meeting the day before in Mr Kabir's office and had sent her family members instead. Sia kept looking at her and she felt for a brief second that their eyes met. Or perhaps she wished they met. But then, the lady seemed too lost in her own thoughts to see Sia and the next of what Sia saw, the woman had started chanting some mantra/prayer softly.

She suddenly seemed short of breath and the man in the blue jacket (*who Sia figured was infact her nephew as he addressed her as bua ji*) took out the inhaler from her jhola and handed it out to her. The local lawyer requested for a chair to be brought for her client given her condition and ill health. That he had to virtually ask twice for it and the same was not given by default was something which agitated Sia.

By now, everyone's focus including Sia's was completely on her. The lady was now finally facing the Magistrate and Mr Kabir was standing next to her. Two hefty looking men were standing on their right and Sia saw two men (assuming her sons) standing there as well.

The Hon'ble Magistrate looked at Mr Kabir and asked,

"Mr Mehta is your client ready?", to which he looked at her client and said a soft Yes My Lord. The Hon'ble Magistrate then asked the opposite lawyers whether they are ready with the questions to which they replied a rather loud ***"Jee Janaab" (Yes My Lord)***.

Now, as the rules suggest, while the cross-examination is going on, the plaintiff's own lawyer cannot utter a single word (*unless directed to the contrary*) or it would amount to him putting words in his client's mouth and assisting the client which is not permitted as per law.

As Sia thought more and more about it, she could not help but fear how the poor old day was going to face this humungous task at hand.

The cross-examination had finally begun and it was the first time that Sia was attending it.

The old lady was made to sit in a chair at a side where the Court Reader could hear them out easily. The Hon'ble Magistrate began by saying ;

"Mata ji, hum aapse kuch sawal karenge, ghabraiyega mat aur har sawaal ko dhyaan se suniyega aur soch kar jawab dijiega".

(Madamji, we will be asking you few questions, do not worry and think about every question carefully before answering it.)

She was encircled and crowded from everywhere possible. Her own lawyers including Mr Kabir on the left, the Reader and Hon'ble Magistrate in the front, the two opposite lawyers alongwith their clients on her right. It came to light that the case was filed by the lady against her own sons which seemed bizarre. The young boys sons had not even wished their mother which was a dreary sight.

Was money so powerful and necessary, Sia wondered. All along, she could not feel but utter pity at the lady and fury at her children for putting her in such a disgraceful and helpless situation.

From where Sia was standing, hidden amidst the rush of litigants, she could not even see the proceedings properly and Mr Kabir somehow noticing her uneasiness suddenly prompted her to come in the front besides him. Sia got up from her seat and stood in the front albeit behind Mr Kabir.

The cross examination finally started. Due to paucity of time, the Hon'ble Magistrate began calling out other matters in the hope that the lawyers would do their job pretty well and he did not have to focus completely upon them. (*Later in every court room she went, this seemed to be the norm*).

But, could one really trust the lawyers? With so much of noise and so many lawyers speaking at the same time, how would the poor lady even hear what was being asked to her? Alas, her worst fears were going to come true.

The lady was being asked questions which were literally thrown towards her like a Lasith Malinga bouncer minute after minute. Her age and condition was not relevant to the opposite lawyers at all. The lawyers had to do their job and it seemed they had come with a mission to win this battle for the day atleast, come what may. In between, Sia could see the lady remove her specs, stop those tears which were about to shed with the pallu of her saree, try to speak a few words and with much effort and wait move on with the next question.

To make matters worse, in that span of 10 minutes itself, the opposite lawyers were often raising their tone and warning Mr Kabir not to meddle in between and assist her client, even though to Sia's knowledge, he was not doing anything unlawful. Mr Kabir, the man he was, remained very much solemn and chose to not to say anything unless required and yet there were allegations against him for interfering with the cross examination.

The Hon'ble Magistrate was so occupied with the hundreds of matters listed on the particular day that he had no option but to divert his attention to the other cases. In between, he kept telling Mr Mehta addressing him as Sir considering he was senior in age to let the cross examination happen smoothly.

It was 1.30 pm, it had been one hour, since the endless cross examination which had crossed 65 questions by now. The lady asked for water frequently and she seemed exhausted physically and mentally of course. Not just her, everyone seemed to wait for this case to come to a conclusion and waited with bated breath when the Magistrate would defer the remaining cross to another day or instruct the opposite counsel to restrict the questions.

After the 65th question was over, little did anyone know what the next question would lead to in the court room.

"Question no. 66"

'Mrs Sharma, So, how old was the lease deed in this case?' asked one of the opposite counsels.

The old lady looked below, her head down for few minutes as if trying to recollect, and then suddenly her expression changed perhaps on recalling the answer and stated in a low tone.

"Beta, **निन्यानवे** *('Ninyaanve/ 99')*

For the utter simple reason of convenience of the court, the next moment, Sia heard her senior lawyer Mr Kabir Mehta repeat his client's answer answer for the reader/ typist to type it and further added that

"Sir my client said 99".

With these three words, all hell seemed to break loose. The opposite lawyers became red with fury as if someone had hit them on the wrong nerve or perhaps as if they were waiting for something like this to happen. Fully charged, they stood up,making Sia perplexed as well as tensed.

One of the opposite lawyers started arguing an octave much higher than before;

'**Mr Mehta,** *Aapne 99 kaise kaha, apko humne itni baar kaha ki aap kuch nahi kahaenge, jab mataji ne ninyaanve kaha toh aap kyu bole'*

(Mr Mehta, how could you say 99, we have told you many times that you shall not prompt your client. When she said ninyanve, then why did you intervene?)

By then, it seemed Mr Mehta was also losing his patience as for the first time, she heard his voice a bit louder than before;

'My Lord, I really fail to comprehend what is the difference between the two? Look at my client. This poor lady is not well versed with English and hence said it in hindi. I just translated it into English for the court's convenience to record it. How does it lead to me influencing her or trying to tell her what to say?'

The other lawyers in a much angry tone and by now filled with rage and disgust for some strange reason had lost their temper.

"Nahi vakeel sahib, aap limit cross kar rahe hain, Judge sahab dekh rahe hain kaise aap har baar beech mein kuch na kuch keh rahe hain. They continued;

Ab aap unhe bolne dijiye, aap 99 kyun keh rahe hain, aap 99 keh kaise sakte hain?"

(No Mr Counsel, you are crossing your limit. Your honour is watching everything. How you are saying something or the other everytime. Why don't you let the lady talk. Why did you mention 99, how could you infact mention it?)

The scene had attracted attention from everyone

present in the court room even by standers and the other proceedings had come to a halt. Like a bollywood shooting scene, everyone stood with bated breath as to what would happen next. The court room was fully packed. There was pin drop silence, which was usually a rarity in the lower courts. Amidst all this, it seemed everyone had forgotten about the old lady.

Perhaps tired of all this irrelevant argument, Mr Kabir had simply had enough. He moved towards one of the opposite lawyers and suddenly in a tone much higher than before, he stated;

"I am telling you my friend please tell your colleague to keep quiet. I have been bearing him for the past one hour. He has made a mockery of this cross examination. He is asking questions beyond the plaint and I am not being allowed to even object it since Hon'ble Magistrate told me not to intervene.

"I request your friend to remain calm and maintain the decorum. What kind of advocacy are we practicing here? Have you even seen my client properly. For the sake of humanity please stop this", he went on as if a volcano inside him silent for long had just erupted. And it had erupted violently and with all its force. Sia was shocked to see this side of her senior and somewhat proud than ever that she was working with this gentleman.

All this was happening in front of the Honourable Magistrate who finally decided to intervene. He seemed much younger than the lawyers themselves. He was recently appointed as the Magistrate of this court and he looked as baffled than others. But he felt clueless as to how to bring the situation in control. Both sides were speaking at the same time now. There was a blank expression on his face.

The lawyers' voices echoed in the whole room and everyone's attention was fixed on these few people. The Magistrate tried to calm the lawyers down but deep inside, he also knew that this was common specially in this part of the country and him raising his voice would only stretch the argument further. He decided to stop the cross examination immediately and was going to ask the Reader to fix another date.

All this was the first time for Sia. She never imagined court room proceedings could be this amusing and extreme and would lead to such unpredictable scenarios.

Sia had also been so totally engrossed in this drama that had unfolded that she suddenly remembered and looked towards the old lady. She was looking down, no one was bothered about how she was feeling, whether she was able to sit on an uncomfortable chair or not. Whether she needed some water, or even more fresh air considering she was squeezed in from all sides. No one was interested whether the sounds of the lawyers gave her a headache. Whether she even could sit there or wanted to go home.

Everyone was rather too happy in the free entertainment they had just got, it seemed, that they had forgotten the basic tenets of humanity by watching an old helpless lady in a condition like this. The arguments went on and on until the Hon'ble Magistrate took the matters in his own hands, stated firmly to the lawyers of the opposite party to calm down, looked at his monitor and saw the questions particularly the question no. 66 which had led to all this commotion.

To settle the confusion once and for all, the old lady was asked again, this time in a much softer tone by the Hon'ble Magistrate himself;

'Aapne kya kaha tha mataji, kitne saal?'

(what did you mention madam, how many years?)

She raised her head, looked at him, then to the opposite lawyers and with moist eyes replied;

"Judge sahib, maine ninyaanve kaha tha aur mere vakil sahab ne 99, bas itna hi."

(My lord, I had said ninyaanve and my lawyer had said 99, that is all)

This time, she got up from the chair herself without letting anyone touch her, and with the help of her stick started walking out of the court room. She had left the cross examination in the middle and ofcourse not even the Judge himself at that moment had any power to stop her or had the courage to tell her to wait. Each face in the room turned 45 degrees left as she made her way out.

The Hon'ble Magistrate not knowing what to do simply stated that since it is lunch time let the matter be taken up two weeks from today for the remaining cross-examination. With a saddened look on his face, he rose up from his seat and left the room. He did not take up any matter post this case in the other half of the day. Soon, the others followed including the lady's sons with no remorse on their faces. On the other hand, the men in white kurtas and the man in blue Nehru jacket walked fast towards the old lady only Mr Kabir and Sia remaining inside the court room

Sia didn't even realize the tears which had started flowing down her cheeks. She had felt like getting up from her seat and helping the lady but she just could not take the first step. She looked at her senior lawyer Mr Kabir Mehta who was still sitting with his head down, his right hand holding a pen which he flicked continuously. Sia knew now why Mr Kabir had agreed for appearing in this particular case.

She also knew another thing for sure, she would never be able to erase the memory of this cross examination from her mind ever.

******

"The Court"

"Cursus Curiae est lex Curiae"

"The practice of the Court is the Law of the Court"

2. The Kid on the Last Bench

31ˢᵗ October 2011,

10.30 am, District Courts

"**W**ake up Sia, its already 8.45am!!" Don't you have to go to the court today? Hurry up beta", shouted her mom from the other end in the kitchen while Sia lay asleep in the bed dreading having to face another challenging day ahead.

The last night was supposed to be pretty exciting for her as she had managed to get a cam print of the recently released movie "Ra One" from her friend and could not wait to watch it. An ardent SRK fan as she was, the wait for being able to watch his new movie was finally over. However, the movie did not turn out as expected once again and his choice of movies lately was making her furious and dejected at the same time.

She had been up till 1am in the morning to somehow finish the movie and had dozed off in the last few minutes of the movie itself. She had also been up for another reason. It was her younger sister's birthday and she had stayed awake bearing the movie so she could wish her sis as the clock struck midnight. Her sister had slept by then and her phone call woke her up with a jolt. Instead of thanking her, she rather told Sia a thing or two for disturbing her sleep which irritated Sia and it had spoilt her night anyway.

And now, the sound of her mother startled her as she emerged from her rather unusual dream of interviewing SRK at his home in Bandra and reality hit her as she saw the clock strike 9am.

"Shit, I gotta rush" she stormed out of bed running straight to the loo while telling her mom to pack her breakfast lest she ends up in a traffic jam once again.

It was the usual routine mundane court day, she had to reach the court by 10 am as all district court rooms mostly commenced the proceedings by 10.15-10.30 am. She told the auto wallah to drive fast as they crossed the heavy traffic of Delhi specially the Ring Road while praying to God that the Hon'ble Magistrate might also be stuck in the same rush hour which had become the defining element of the city of Delhi lately.

She was currently working under a lawyer based in South Delhi who was a family dispute specialist. She was no fan of being a part of divorce and similar proceedings but she was keen on taking some experience in this branch of law as well which was always sought after.

Her lawyer, Mr Aditya Sharma was a young lad in his early thirties but had earned quite a name in the profession. His areas of practice included lower courts and High Court. He also took up other civil law matters off and on. It was only a six month assignment she had taken on and she had made this clear to Mr Aditya in the beginning of her training itself. She browsed through the case file once again on the way in the auto while the auto wallah drove as fast as he could to make her reach on time. Now well versed with court proceedings, Sia was beginning to enjoy this profession. This particular matter had her attention and she was thorough with the case at hand. Mr Aditya was a very supportive person who was very encouraging towards buddying lawyers and involved Sia in this case at the nascent stages itself.

It was a Petition for Judicial Separation under Sec 10 of the Hindu Marriage Act and they were representing the husband who had filed the petition against his wife on the grounds of desertion. The couple also had a six year old son who was currently residing with his mother.

Apparently, the wife was not interested in cohabiting with the husband in the initial months after the marriage itself but was continuing due to pressure from both the elder members of the families. She always wanted to work abroad and their client was fully supportive of her decision but once she went for an assignment in South East Asia, she distanced herself from her husband altogether. Unable to bear the separation and insecure of losing his wife, Sia's client Madhav left his secure and stable respected government job, moved to the country where his wife Sunita was and for a brief period of time things started to resume to normalcy.

Or maybe they appeared to be so. Sabir was born and they became parents. Thinking this to be the apt time, Madhav tried to convince his wife to return to India for some time atleast so that their parents could get to see their grandson. She eventually agreed but perhaps it was a decision she had taken half heartedly and no one had a clue as to what was in her mind.

When their son Sabir was two years old, one fine day she packed her bags and left their home leaving no trace of her whereabouts. To add to his grief, she took their son alongwith him and for the last three years, Madhav had not even seen his son nor spoken to him. Left with no option, he was advised to resort to legal proceedings to end this marriage which had already failed long way back.

Despite several summons issued to the opposite party, the lady had neither appeared herself before the court nor through her lawyer. The Court had fixed this day as the last and final chance for the wife to make an appearance or it would proceed ex-parte i.e. in the presence of one party only.

It was a normal day for Sia as by now she was used to the daily grind in a lower court. She would accompany her lawyer to the concerned court, return to office by 4pm, prepare for the matters listed on the next day and in between do some drafting of applications/ replies if given to her by her senior. Though the cases involved application of mind and law, she used to get disturbed over reading about failed marriage cases which were rising in the country lately and often carried the baggage home as well.

She had no clue what this day would bring for her and little did she know that the happenings of 31.10.2011 would remain etched in her memory for reasons which were about to be revealed.

She reached the Court premises and almost ran to the court no. 10 where their matter was listed as Item No. 13. Their client was already present in the court premises and was speaking to her senior Mr. Aditya in a rather solemn manner.

She joined the conversation and it was seeming a rather remote possibility that his wife would appear today as well as he had gathered from his sources that she had left the country recently and gone to Malaysia.

The Hon'ble Magistrate entered the court room and everyone became silent and rose in respect. Sia had particular admiration for this Judge who was a young

Metropolitan Magistrate of the batch of 2009 and was a strict disciplinarian particularly in terms of punctuality. He was known for declining adjournments on frivolous grounds and had a record of passing orders within 6-7 months in most cases. Perhaps, he would decide to proceed ex parte today, thought Sia.

While Item No. 1 was being called, their client stood up and went towards the exit of the courtroom perhaps to attend a phone call. But the moment he returned, Sia could see that his face had turned red and his usual calm expression had turned into an anxious one. He rushed towards Mr Aditya and both their faces turned towards the left.

Before Sia could start guessing what could be the reason she saw a lady enter the room along with a small lean spectacled boy who seemed to have held onto his mother tightly. It did not take long for Sia to realize that the client's wife had decided to make an appearance after all. But she was surprised on seeing the boy and was unable to fathom why would his mother want their kid to be a witness to such a proceeding. She did not know then that she would know the answer real soon.

Looking at them, Madhav and Mr Aditya exchanged few words which from a distance seemed more like her senior trying to comfort their client. Sia stood at a distance and thought it better not to meddle in their conversation. Seeing his son after so long was bound to bring out all the pent up emotions in Madhav.

Sia had read the file over and over but was unable to understand the exact reason as to why had his wife

Mrs Sunita had deserted her family like this. Why was she unhappy? Was there someone else in her life? Was she being harassed and their client had not revealed the full details? As always she had innumerable questions in her mind which sought answers.

But from what Sia had gauged about her client during past meetings, he came across as a thorough gentleman who was very polite, courteous and respectful towards everyone the opposite gender in particular. He seemed like an honest, simple, sobre man. What could he have possibly done wrong or done right to save this marriage? She had begun to feel pity for him after initial few meetings itself.

And now while Sia was looking at Madhav, she realized that despite the month of October and the air conditioned court room, the poor man was sweating. And sweating bad. She also observed his teary eyes as he was looking at his child craving a hug or atleast a smile in return.

He continued to stare at his son who almost jumped on seeing his father after so long only to be curtailed by his mother who pushed him and held him tight enough to make him sit on a bench in the last row alongwith him forcing him to put his head down and remain silent. Sia was already disgusted with what she had just witnessed and this was one court proceeding she hoped she was not a part of already.

Item No. 13 finally called. The Hon'ble Magistrate as everyone else was rather surprised on seeing the opposite party finally appearing in the matter along with their lawyer. At the first instance itself, he imposed heavy costs upon them for the rather unreasonable delay in bringing the matter to its logical conclusion and wasting the time of the court and of the other party.

Upon being questioned by the judge, Mrs Sunita in a rather soft tone, stated that she had been out of the country and was unable to get leaves from her ongoing assignment and hence could not make appear for the proceedings early on. The Hon'ble Magistrate asked further questions and gave their lawyer an opportunity to get their statement recorded to which he prompted his client Mrs Sunita to state her version.

The usual back bencher Sia was somehow more upfront in this matter and decided to experience things first hand and stood in the front alongwith her client and Mr Aditya While the Hon'ble Magistrate was browsing through the case file, as Mrs Sunita started her version of the story, the next visual shocked not just Sia but almost everyone present in the court room.

Suddenly, Mrs Sunita turned around and called her son Sabir sitting at the bench in the last row;

"beta idhar aajao, aage aao" (Son, come here , in the front).

Sabir, a young boy dressed in blue jeans and white shirt looked completely blank and was frozen for a second. Since he had entered the court room he had been in a state of utter helplessness. He was too young to understand what was this place and why was he brought there. As surprised he was to see his father he did not know why there were so many other people along with his parents. At that time all he wanted was his mom dad, his world, to be with him. He wished for them to all stay together like one happy family and was desperate to be held by his father.

Kids though small have a mind of their own. With all these thoughts running in his mind, he seemed reluctant to get up from his seat. Mrs Sunita noticing his hesitance, this time called him out again with a much angrier tone and as if out of fear the poor kid rose up and slowly came in front of the Magistrate. While the Magistrate was busy answering a query of the reader regarding the contents of the proceeding's order which she was typing, Sia observed something unusual and shocking. Mrs Sunita in a hushed tone, coerced her son to hold her arm tight and pretend to be weeping. She almost heard the words very clearly

"Just for a few minutes beta don't you want to go to Disneyland with Mumma this year? Don't look at Daddy you know na he never came to meet you all this while. Now this Judge Uncle will only let us go for our trip if we win today and now you listen to Mumma and start crying."

The boy looked at her mother and tears started to fall from his eyes. But for some reason those tears did not seem fabricated. Coming from a young boy's eyes, they seemed as genuine and pure as anything. His eyes displayed an emotion which was saddening. The boy himself took out a handkerchief from his right pocket of his jeans and tried to wipe them.

Sia was startled. What was this woman up to? Was she completely devoid of any emotions? The institution of marriage in which she firmly believed in was crumbling day by day in a dismal manner.

What would the poor boy be going through, she wondered. She almost wanted to tell the Hon'ble Magistrate what she had heard but it she doubted if she could interfere in this manner. The Hon'ble Magistrate was busy looking at the monitor and was oblivious to what was happening in his court room, (*or so she assumed*). She looked at her client who was standing with his head down. She looked at Mr Aditya who was busy browsing through the documents. She looked at Mrs Sunita and she felt she saw a faint smile on her face. She almost hated where she was standing and again prayed this proceeding to get over soon. And the next moment something happened which startled everyone present there.

After about five minutes when the boy was standing still with his mother, the Hon'ble Magistrate removed his glance from the monitor, closed the file put in front of him looked straight towards the parties standing in front of him and asked the opposite party's counsel:

"My dear friend, are you a novice lawyer? How long have you been in practice?" He asked with a rather firm aggressive tone.

The lawyer, bit hesitant adjusted his tie, fumbled with the documents in his hand and answered in a perplexed tone:

"No my lord I have been practicing for the past seven years."

The Hon'ble judge then looked at Sabir and said:

"Beta why don't you please go out and wait for your mother to come, she will join you soon", he pointed at the court clerk to accompany the kid to the bench kept outside the room and told him firmly to remain seated with him until further orders.

The kid somewhat confused and tad relieved, wiped his face once again with his left hand, gave one last look at both his parents and left the room immediately.

The Hon'ble Magistrate then asked Mrs Sunita;

"Mam you know this is a case filed by your husband for judicial separation right?

"Umm yes sir, came the reply",from the lady

"I hope your lawyer had told you and briefed you in advance regarding the purpose of your presence in the court today?"

"I guess so My Lord", she was getting anxious

"You are aware that today's proceeding was not related to the question of the custody of your child right?", Hon'ble Magistrate's tone was getting more firm now.

"Yes I know Sir", both she and her lawyer were now feeling nervous and looking at each other blankly.

The Magistrate almost rose from his chair to say the next words;

"Then Mam why did you bring your child into this place? I have been noticing you since the moment you entered my court. You avoid accepting summons for the past three months

and when you finally decide to grace us with your presence you bring your child along?"

The Hon'ble Magistrate had noticed the entire proceedings word by word it seemed.

"No sir, I thought to bring him inside, did not know where else to." She almost cut him in between only to face a much angrier tone from the other end now.

"No Madam you do not, and I repeat you simply do not bring small innocent children into court rooms unless the judge specifically calls for them himself. And what were you trying to achieve by telling your kid to come in front of me and shed some tears? I do not know who is guilty for the failure of your marriage and I shall not opine on it unless I hear both parties out but I am shocked at how you are trying to use your own son as a pawn to tilt this case in your favour? Do you even realize what kind of impact would it leave on your son's mind and conscience?

The lady thoroughly embarrassed on hearing all this simply stood frozen and there was an eerie silence in the room.

Deep inside Sia was feeling not really happy but rather reprieved at the fact that the judge was not oblivious to everything after all. He might have been busy in other matters but his eyes and ears were everywhere in this room.

The judge as if realizing he had almost lost his cool in front of a large audience drank a glass of water kept on his table and said:

"I repeat and I repeat again for all of you present in the court room, none of you shall make your children witness to court proceedings like what just happened today in front of me." He looked at everyone as if addressing a class full of students. He continued;

"And Madam, if you try to do this one more time, I am going to proceed ex parte despite you being present and shall hold you in contempt of this court and all of this could go really adverse to your matter."

With the above words he looked at the reader and dictated

"Please record- ***Opposite party Mrs Sunita Verma present today. Statement not recorded. Costs of Rs 20,000/- for delay in appearance to be paid to Legal Aid Services Authority today. Matter adjourned for 7th Dec 2011.***

Court breaks for ten minutes.

With this, he rose from his chair and left the room leaving everyone stunned.

For a minute, the court room remained silent. Slowly, the lawyers and others started leaving the room. Sia picked up her bag and bunch of files and looked at their client Madhav who was standing in a corner. Mrs Sunita was standing in the other corner of the room. Everyone else had left.

And then, Sia looked at the door and was shocked to see young Sabir standing there. The expressions on his face made it aptly clear that he was there all this while. He was looking at his mother and his father both. He was crying, and this time again, the tears were real. Sia felt like embracing him but decided against it. She tried to hide the tears falling down from her eyes.

She thought it best to leave the family alone. Before leaving she looked at the seat of the Hon'ble Magistrate, she felt more and more respect for this young judge.

She wondered why it was said that the law is blind. It was neither blind nor deaf after all.

******

The Case

"Lex non deficere potest in jusitia exhibenda"

"The law cannot fail in dispensing justice"

3. The wait for Item No. 25.

*"S*ia, *our matter is in the Regular List in the High Court since 1998 and it can be heard anyday anytime now"*, told Sia's new Boss, the Head of Legal Dept of the company she had recently joined, as he informed her that she was supposed to visit the High Court the next day post 2 pm.

Sia had finally achieved some sort of stability in her legal career and had landed up her first long term work assignment. It was a one year contractual job in a private company in their in-house law department based in a city in

North India. This offer had come as a random opportunity through a cousin's reference and she had applied for it without any intention of joining in case selected.

The reason was that she did not want to join a so soon and restrict herself to legal cases of a particular company only neither was interested in clerical work. She had begun to look forward to visiting courts and despite the endless wait in the court rooms and erratic work timings, it was captivating enough for her. She was not so keen on a desk job and felt there was a lot more which she had to learn in this profession in case she wished to start her own practice in some time.

But, unlike other internships/trainings which rarely paid a penny or paid some very few bucks, she was going to be paid Rs 30,000/- per month for her stint in this company which was further extendable upon expiration of the one year term. Compared to her friends and other batchmates, she was getting a real decent deal.

After two rounds of interview, first with the senior Management and the second one with the Head of the Company himself, she had been one out of the 3 officers selected for the position of Law Trainee, Luckily, she was being given the position in a city in North India and it was a one hour daily commute from her cousin's place to the office. She had resisted the offer at first and was reluctant with a 9-5 job, but ultimately she gave in after being convinced by her family that this could be a new beginning for her and could provide the stability her career desperately needed.

It had been one month since she had joined her new office and the initial period had been rather uneventful. After the initial rounds of introductions, her first two weeks were spent in interactions with the various other departments of the company. She was briefed on the kinds of legal cases filed by and against the Company and what would be her role and responsibilities. There were two more officers in their team, one male and one female and she was the youngest out of the lot.

Since she had already been actively involved in court proceedings earlier, her new Boss sensed it and also thought it best to make her acquainted with the cases of the company first hand. He decided to send her to the High court for this particular matter which had been pending for last ten years for final hearing. The case was quite simple.

It was a very old writ petition filed by her company against its rejection in technical bid and non-allotment of the tender by a PSU. It had been alleged that their bid was wrongly rejected for want of certain original documents while the tender conditions stated that certified true copies of the documents shall also be validly accepted.

The said matter, after being admitted in 1998 had not been heard thereafter and had been put in the regular list. Despite mentioning it several times before the Hon'ble Court, it could not be taken up most times as the courts were over burdened with daily matters itself.

With this background, Sia was handed over the file and was instructed to come to office the next day and go to the High Court after lunch as a representative on behalf of the Company and contact her panel advocate upon reaching there.

Half-heartedly, Sia accepted this new assignment knowing fully well that she had no power to reject this not so wonderful offer in the initial period of her career itself. Till now she had never spent more than 3-4 months at any particular training be it any organization or under an Advocate. But as strictly told by her parents, she was supposed to linger on in this job for atleast one year.

The day coming to a tad disappointing end, she reached home and simply resigned into her room hoping the new day brings some exciting challenges for her. But a phone conversation with her college mate dashed all her hopes. She was not so much aware then about what the Regular List was and had earlier found it awkward asking her Boss about it since she feared being mocked at for not being aware of it. Hence, she had called up her friend that night only to be told that she was venturing into virtually a dead zone. During the half an hour conversation, she was saddened to realize that considering the fact that the matter was in the Regular list, the next day and perhaps the days and weeks coming ahead were going to be as futile as it can get,

"Why is it called a Regular List then?!" she hung up and asked herself thinking about what her friend had just told her. He explained to her the terms Advance, Supplementary and Regular Lists and the mother of these lists, the CAUSE LIST which governed an advocate's career heavily.

So each evening post 4 pm, the respective courts particularly High Courts and Supreme Courts would publish the cause list for the next day on their website and it would be on display at the court as well. Cause List simply meant cumulatively the list of cases fixed for hearing court wise on a particular day. Besides, one can see only the advance list and supplementary list separately as well.

All the fresh matters/applications/petitions filed perhaps few days or even a day before were listed first thing in the morning and were grouped as Supplementary List. Next, came the Advance List, which contained matters which have already been listed earlier atleast once and are now coming up on their scheduled date of hearing for further proceedings as fixed by the Court. And then came the Regular List which contained old matters of perhaps decade back or years ago which have been categorized into this list.

She was explained that once a matter was categorized to be listed in the Regular List, there was no way one could even remotely predict when it would be listed. Regular matters were listed as per their date of admission or institution and were not heard on priority by the courts unless there was some urgency required. Unfortunately, this list comes up for hearing only when a respective court has finished hearing matters of the other two lists.

 Upon knowing this, Sia was shocked and disheartened at the same time. She was further told that in most cases it would take a long time for this list to be taken up unless an application for early hearing is filed and accepted by the court and only few judges specifically fixed time slots say post lunch to specially hear these Regular Matters.

As luck would have it, the court where her matter was listed was infact taking up Regular List post 2 pm almost each day. Forcing herself to feel some positivity within, next day she got ready and left for the office and later to the Court only with the hope that perhaps she might get more lucky and her case might be taken up in the coming week itself. She did not tell anyone but she did pack a small novel in her bag just in case she would have to spend the entire afternoon sitting inside the court premises doing perhaps nothing.

As she reached the court around 1.30pm and walked inside the lobby, Sia sensed the same vibes which came from visiting similar other courts. As usual, it was buzzing with activity, literally buzzing with all hustle bustle as if the people of the entire city had some legal case here. Sia had come after a long time to any Court and before that had come to the High Court only a couple of times.

Sia looked left, looked right and as far as she could see, there were young girls and boys, middle aged men, women and some very aged advocates, all dressed up in black and white, collars, robes, holding files and most were well dressed. Almost everyone appeared to be in some sort of mad rush, few literally running to their respective court rooms bumping into her and ignoring everything and anything that came along their way.

Each time Sia entered a court room she used to be amazed at the number of lawyers around her. From where did all these lawyers pass out from? She used to be fascinated at the charged up atmosphere where half of the advocates had only come for mere passovers and adjournments and perhaps only a selected few cases would be brought to their logical conclusion on a particular day. Yet, be it the number of cases or the number of advocates, they just seemed to increase manifold each passing day.

Sia put these thoughts away and began walking towards the court. The atmosphere was so full of energy that she began to compare it with her dull monotonous days at the new office where she spent almost her entire day sitting on a chair in front of a computer. There was such a stark difference in the two environments. Sia could easily understand why young budding lawyers went in for litigation(court practice) instead of a cushy 9-5 corporate or government job. But she did not know then whether she was cut out for it or not.

She waited for the clock to strike 2pm since it was lunch time and then reached her respective court room on the first floor. As the first two-three rows were meant for advocates, Sia found a place in the second last row and sat there waiting desperately for her matter to be called at the earliest. Not that she really expected that to happen on the first day itself. After last night's conversation with her friend, she was pretty sure this was going to be her daily schedule for the coming days and had resigned to her fate dejectedly.

The advocate who was representing her company was a 75 year old man accompanied with a junior lawyer whom she met just outside the court room. To make matters worse, it was brought to her knowledge that the reason for a delay in their matter being heard was that there was a decade old family property dispute which was listed just before their matter and which was taking ages to conclude.

That matter was at the stage of final arguments since many months. But considering the stake involved, her company could not take any chances and someone had to be definitely present on behalf of her company and carry the relevant original file containing the documents the court might refer or wish to see during the course of final arguments.

While she sat in the second last row in the surprisingly extremely chilled air conditioner, very soon she felt time had come to a standstill. As the clock struck 3 pm and then slowly 4 pm, it was the decade old property matter which continued for those two hours. There were three lawyers representing each side of the party and it seemed they had a lot a lot to say and argue in the matter.

A couple of times, Sia dozed off only to realize she might be noticed by the judge and had to resort to looking down and pretending to be reading her case file while she was reading the "*The Hungry Tide*", an Amitav Ghosh book. Not a big fan of cool rooms since they gave her frequent headaches, she wondered why was the Air conditioner at such a low temperature. Was she the only one freezing out there, she felt with a tinge of disgust. A coat or stole had to be carried from next day onwards she firmly told herself. She received calls from her office few times only to be told to keep sitting there till the judge himself did not call it a day.

As hours passed and the court concluded the proceedings for the day around 4.30 pm, Sia was thoroughly and heavily bored. It annoyed her that her lawyer had left in between and upon enquiring from his junior, she was told he had an important matter in another court to attend to which subdued her frustration a bit. She had become irritated at the futility of the entire day and felt blank as she walked towards the exit gate carrying the hefty case file back with her only to bring it back the next day.

The day had ended and Sia reached home by 5.30 pm. She reflected on the day that went by only to smile at the fact that she had simply done nothing besides typing a reply to legal notice in the morning before coming to the court and reading 30 pages of her novel.

Little did she know that this was going to be her schedule for the next three weeks to come. Each day in the morning she would go to the office, read some case file, make some notes if required, vet some MOUs which were rather rarely given to her and after eating her lunch leave for the Court at 1.15pm.

Each afternoon, she would reach the court room with a faint hope that perhaps today through some divine intervention her matter might be heard and she would be free from this particular one case which had turned into a mission impossible by then. Was she being paid for sitting in a court room half of her day and simply hearing people talk? She used to ponder. Was this the norm everywhere?

She often used to bump into her batchmates in the court and would see most of them either rushing to a court to take a Passover or carrying files behind their seniors, or some others working under a judge taking notes as he passed his daily orders. Only a few among those she knew were actually getting a chance to plead before a court or were doing some quality legal drafting work. The pointlessness of her daily activity disgusted her to the core. Sia had never felt so helpless in her entire life uptil then. She tried her best to concentrate on the arguments of the lawyers in the property dispute but their voices were so low and the issue seemed so complicated that she would lose interest in fifteen minutes itself.

Sometimes Sia got interested in their legal points specially when the judge asked them to explain a certain provision or cite a relevant judgment. Other times she just looked around at the people who were affected by what order the judge would pass, the uneasy, anxious look on their faces and she felt sympathetic towards them. Perhaps, there was a hidden purpose in all of this, she used to ask herself. Whether she learnt the nuances of law in those three weeks she did not know but she definitely did learn a thing or two about patience being the biggest virtue in this period of time.

To her surprise and perhaps to give her moral support, her *75 year old lawyer* would always remain seated inside the court room in the front row patiently listening to the lawyers arguing in front barring 1-2 occassions when he had to leave for loo break or for some other urgent hearing. Though he also knew there was a rare chance of their matter being heard, but Sia found some inspiration and solace in the fact that he was also going through the same ordeal as her that too at such an old age.

If he could do it, so could she. Each day, both of them would enter the court room by almost the same time, exchange wishes and then sit at their respective seats for the next 2 hours or sometimes more with nothing absolutely nothing to look forward to.

The only saviour for Sia, in this otherwise beautiful court was its Canteen. Ask anyone and everyone who has ever visited this court, he/she would never leave without eating something at the canteen or café as its also famously called. During her previous internships, Sia had visited it 1-2 times and was amazed to see its diverse menu; the naan, panner, biryani, idli, dosa, chicken, samosa, pastry, fresh juice and so on.

As usual, it was fully occupied and there seemed no empty seat on any given day. The waiters were always running around with steaming hot delicacies and the unique and amusing thing about them was that they carried absolutely no pens and papers. The only part of the court devoid of the usage of a pen/pencil and paper was this famous canteen. No matter how much the crowd, they just orally took the orders and they somehow always remembered what was to be served at which table.

And now that Sia was a regular visitor, she would often come early and savour the delicacies so it would give her some impetus to be able to bear the rest of day in her court room.

30.09.2013

High Court, 16:00 hrs

"Item Number 25"

This sound brought Sia back to reality with a sudden jolt. While she was recalling the taste of the butter chicken and naan she had just relished, the number 25 almost made her jump from her seat. With almost four weeks now spending her afternoons inside the court room waiting for her matter to be called out one divine day, Sia could not imagine what this moment would mean for her.

It all happened too soon for her to fathom what was going on there. The arguments in the previous dispute were going on since 2.30pm and it was the opposite party/ defendant's counsel (the defendant being the one who was charged with an offence) to say his side of the story. Like each day, Sia knew nothing fruitful would happen and by 4.30pm the Hon'ble judge would call it a day. But as it came to light, apparently, the judge became so weary of listening to so much of a particular issue since so many days that he told the defendant's counsel to get some more latest judgments.

The Hon'ble Judge deferred that matter to another day in the same month as the counsel had requested for a short date. He had called out the next case number and was keen on disposing it off on that day itself since it had been lingering on for a long time and he had read the case well and did not seem a complicated issue to him.

Time stood still once again for Sia, but this time she felt as if she had finally won her ticket to freedom. As if she had won a huge lottery. Her eyes became wide with attention and she braced herself and stood up and hurriedly went to stand next to her senior counsel who was usually seated in the first row itself assuming he might have got up by now to come in front.

As Sia literally pushed the sea of people aside and reached the first row, she heard the sound Item No. 25 glaring into her ears once again only to realize that her lawyer, her one constant companion for past three and a half weeks was *nowhere within her sight!!!*

She looked around the entire court room, there was no one who looked like her lawyer. She could not even find his junior lawyer inside the room. Sia recalled having met him just after lunch and infact till few minutes back, he was seated in front of her fully in her view. And now she had absolutely no clue where the hell had he vanished? She was nervous, furious and restless at the same time. The wait since so many weeks , this ordeal, this never ending movie was finally reaching its climax but unfortunately her 75 year old savior had decided to leave her alone at the last moment.

Meanwhile, the judge called out this time rather loud for the last time whether anyone was present on behalf of the plaintiff i.e. her company. There was a junior counsel present from the opposite party. Sia fiddled with her phone which was in her hand but she knew she could not use it inside the court room and definitely not standing in front of the Hon'ble Judge himself.

She had already been penalized on one occasion earlier when her cell phone was accidently on ringing mode and the tone had buzzed loud in the court room only to have her phone confiscated by the court reader for the entire day. Not wanting a repeat of that, she now fumbled for words and somehow managed to state that her lawyer would be entering the court room any minute.

Being a trainee and having no general power of attorney in her name, she could not even get her presence recorded inside the court.

Sia kept trying his cell phone again and this time the bell rang but it got cut in few seconds. May be he was on his way back, Sia thought, the worried look on her face slowly vanishing away. However, the judge seemed in an awful mood or simply too tired to wait or listen to what the other counsel was trying to say. And then he started to tell Sia a thing or two on court room discipline, how she was wasting the court's time, how the junior counsel of the opposite party should have been more well-briefed about the matter, and so on.

Sia stood there, silent, simply looking at the Hon'ble Judge with no expression on her face. She wanted to rip her hair off, she wanted to tell him that she was more desperate for this matter to be heard than she had ever been desperate for any damn thing in her life. That she literally did not care whether this case was decided in favour or against her company. She just simply wanted this matter to be OVER at any cost!!

But alas, the judge was not willing to answer her prayers, adjourned the matter for non presence on behalf of plaintiff and called upon Item No. 26 instead. Within the next five minutes, he decided to call it a day. Sia stood aside, still, not knowing what to do or say.

Dejected and madly furious at her lawyer but a bit relieved that the day was over, she came out and bumped into a stout aged man trying to rush inside.

'Sia what happened? Where is everyone going? Is the matter over? Was our matter listed?"

He had literally hurried past the crowd to enter inside and was panting badly while speaking .

"I had another urgent criminal matter in the next court hence I had to rush. But I took a Passover there and came running here. So what happened?

Sia stared at the man trying to make conversation with him and felt more pity for him than herself. It was her lawyer, her poor lawyer who had left the other case only to attend to this one. He was back, but it was already too late. Sia felt a loss of words but mustered up the courage to explain what had happened in the past ten minutes.

'Yes Sir, I can understand your urgency. Yes sir, our matter was called out but the judge did not wait much for us and adjourned it to be taken up for another day", was all Sia could say. Her lawyer seemed equally dejected and scolded his junior who was standing nervously in front of him for informing him so late.

Sia looked at him, wished him good day and left for home. It seemed the wait for the Regular List was to continue for some more time. It also seemed that the word "Regular List" was not be taken on face value. By then Sia's patience got the better of her and she stopped going to her office from the next week itself citing some illness which could take weeks to recover.

Thereafter, she simply stopped going. If this is what court practice entails, she is perhaps not cut out for it, Sia thought. She also made up her mind she was also cut out for a 9-5 job so soon atleast. And so she decided to grab every opportunity that came her way without caring for the financial and stability aspects. She was firm. And this time no one could stop her.....

Few months later, was in the same court one day for another matter, she bumped into her ex colleague from the same company and could not resist a smile upon knowing that the particular judge had got transferred and the new judge was busy taking up new cases. She assumed that her matter would of course be still pending. It was clear that the regular list had not been taken up in the past few months on even a single day.

However, to her surprise, her colleague told that before being transferred, the Hon'ble Judge fixed a date for hearing certain matters in the regular list which were part heard at the stage of final arguments. Fortunately, that very matter was also chosen to be heard by the respected Judge amongst the list. She felt rather relieved that the same old lawyer argued the matter and it was decided in favour of the company she was once a part of. The Hon'ble Judge had directed issuance of the writ of Mandamus (directions) to the concerned PSU to consider the case of her previous company and pass a speaking order. Alas, she thought, the long ardous wait for Item No. 25 was finally over.

The regular list may get tad irregular sometimes but justice was not denied after all....

******

"The Counsel"

"The law speaks to all with one mouth"

"Lex Uno Ore Omnes Alloquitor"

4. Behind Those Dark Shades:

30th August 2013:

Bercos, Connaught place

"So tell me Sia, today its my birthday and you got to tell me now about that man Advocate Mr Sameer Singh, and everything else as well, "asked Sia's best friend one fine day during their lunch date at Bercos, Connaught Place. Sia had just finished her brief stint at a Human Rights related Non Profit Organisation based in Central Delhi. All this while, her best friend Siddharth had only heard her go ga ga about the fact that she had got an opportunity to work with a wonderful lawyer whom she never stopped raving about.

How and where did she meet him? Who was he? And what was so special about him? Sia smiled as she recalled and started speaking finally about the man for the first time after so many years.

The first meeting

The year was 2008 the month - September. Sia was in her final (third) year of Law College and was by then thoroughly bored of the campus, where absolutely nothing happened each day. She had hence involved herself in as many internships and trainings as possible. She had had enough of law firm, court room drama, litigation and was still wondering where she would finally land up.

Continuing with the search for answers to her questions, she had applied for an internship at a Delhi based non-profit organization which worked for a variety of legal, social and human right issues. Sia found this as the perfect platform to experience working in a place, where she would get a chance to deal with legal cases of a different kind. To fight for the common man, the poor, the underprivileged and make their voices heard and she was really excited to go there once she was selected.

On the first day of her training, Sia reached the head office in Central Delhi early morning around 9am, although after lot of asking about strangers and roaming endlessly locating the office address. Finally, she realized she was being directed back to where she had initially stopped her auto and the building she was looking for was right there. But, the office entry was in a small service lane and a small Board was put up which was almost negligible.

Sia climbed up the stairs and entered the first floor. She was welcomed by the HR department and immediately introduced to her work profile. They told that she was being allotted the team which worked on Rights of the Disabled.. Sia was disappointed at first as she was more keen on getting the team working on Prison Rights or Child Rights as she had explored on their website. However, she realized soon that had no say in this and it was already her first day. She was then given a brief of her Sir, her senior, who was going to be her mentor for this one month.

She was then was given a heavy booklet on the Persons with Disabilities Act and the various judgments relating to it. Sia confessed to Siddharth that uptil then she

had never heard of such an Act till that moment which ashamed her as well. Forget it being a part of her course curriculum, she had never heard about it even on TV or in the newspapers. It was like a dead Act, toothless and she wondered how many of even the disabled even about it.

Till her lawyer came back from the meeting, Sia sat in one corner of the room and sleepily tried to turn the endless pages. It was well, a heavy book for a first day in the office. She kept looking at the clock on the wall and waited for hours to pass which seemed eternity. This had been a long day indeed.

She recalled how during lunch break Siddharth had come to meet her at an eating joint near her new workplace and he laughed at remembering how bored she looked at that time.

Back to the story, so just when the day was almost getting over and it was around 4pm, Sia suddenly heard some footsteps. A young boy came up to her, informing her that her senior had finally arrived back and that she was to meet him right then. This young boy was a law student in a college in NCR and was working under him part-time as a part of his legal training.

Relieved and a bit anxious, Sia picked up the books and went upto the second floor where he was seated. Once she came face to face with him, she realized that something was odd. She would understand it later but then, she was in an utterly confused state of mind.

For one, he was pretty younger than she had anticipated, perhaps, late twenties she guessed. He was a bit healthy, dark skinned, but the peculiar feature was that he was wearing **an extremely dark black pair of glasses**. At first, she did not understand why he would really sit in an office wearing those shades. It did seem odd to see someone like that.

But then, it hit her, perhaps he had some flu? She recalled whether she was informed about it, may be it was mentioned to her that he was not keeping well but she could not really remember it. But by then, her mental faculties had stopped responding and she was thinking all sorts of random thoughts in her already cluttered head.

Before she could respond, the young boy brought a jolt to Sia's conscience by telling Sia that his senior, the mentor Sia was going to be attached with for the next one month was *completely visually impaired*. More than anything, Sia was in a state of shock, and she suddenly gasped for breath in a well-ventilated room where she now faced him. *She was not, absolutely not prepared for this.*

Here was a smart looking man, a practicing lawyer who was unfortunately deprived from his vision since childhood. Yet, in her innumerable experiences and meetings so far, Sia had never seen such a confident looking lawyer. She had thousands of questions in her head and curiosity getting the better of her it was very tough to control her mostly talkative tongue.

And now comes the awkward moment which she remembered in detail even to this day. Despite the fact that she now knew he could not see, but suddenly she saw herself getting *conscious, really conscious*. From how she was looking, was she formally dressed, were her hair nicely done, was she standing straight, it went on and on. Just his presence with those eyes covered with those glasses had a powerful *'I can see you'* effect on her. It was tough to understand and comprehend this feeling yet she was experiencing it at that moment. It was weird for sure, and yet, there was something uncanny about those eyes behind the dark shades which only time would tell.

And now that she was standing right before him, Sia really felt as if he could see her. He was observing her every move, every word she uttered, as if he had some magical power with which he could judge her. A part of her was bursting with other questions and was wondering- *How, Just how did he pull it off? How did he become a lawyer? How did he manage to read those endless law books and cases? How does he manage to go to court and argue in front of the judge?* Most importantly, *how the hell does he read up a case and draft the endless pages of applications and petitions that are a lawyer's bread and butter?* Her mind was bursting with such thoughts and more. And the fact that she was to be working under him made her more nervous than excited.

He then introduced himself and it really surprised her to know that he was an alumni of the very law college Sia was a student of. He told me that he had just passed out 2 years back. That made him not so elder to her at all. He had enrolled with the Bar, taken up practice under an individual lawyer and after some experience, had got a job at this NGO.

He told Sia that he was thoroughly enjoying his stint here, working mainly for persons with disabilities, a cause he strongly believed in and few other criminal service matters. He was currently assisting the Head of the organization, on a very serious and important issue,

-relating to granting of certain rights for the hearing disabled in India and the NGO was also in the news for the same.

He seemed very upbeat about being an integral part of the case and wanted to take Sia along to the court in the next hearing. The salary was low as it was a non-profit organization, yet she could feel it that not just him, the other employees as well came across as a dedicated lot, for who money was the last priority.

After that, Sia began talking about herself and answered the questions asked to her about her background and made an extra effort to be cordial and friendly. Something she said brought a smile to his face and once that happened, Sia stared at him again. The Man had such a beautiful smile, she was amazed. It was one of those perfect tv commercials smile, the one which every dentist would love to take credit for, the kinds every one would dream to have.

When he laughed, it lit up his face in a child-like manner and one could sense the innocence in him. She kept looking eerily at his glasses and the eyes behind the dark cover, but she could not see anything. It was probably wrong to expect, yet she wanted him to remove those shades, so that she could look straight into those eyes. She wanted to ask more, but restrained herself as it was only the first meeting.

He told Sia that he even worked on the computer which was great to hear. He had installed a software which could narrate everything he clicked on the internet, everything he typed too. And he had a similar software in his cell phone which would read out the messages and the caller's name as well. Talk about technology benefitting the society in ways rarer than before, but seeing him so self sufficient really made Sia elated.

There was something else brewing up in her mind. Agreed, he was able to use the computer and he could make drafts of cases, edit them, etc. But a case file was a really heavy document and contained lots and lots of pages. For a lawyer to be able to present his case in the court, a single petition was not enough. He had to know the entire facts in detail and be thorough with the supporting documents as well.

It was almost impossible for a visually impaired person to achieve that. And as if he had read her mind and thoughts, he then showed her some white coloured papers which seemed like a huge heavy pile. And then it wasn't difficult to recognize those pages. They were documents in the Braille script, which were nothing but translations of some of his petitions into Braille.

 For this, there were few institutes who would do that for some bucks. It was a cumbersome procedure but the ease with which he showed and explained the process to her, it seemed to Sia that he really enjoyed his profession and worked really really hard for it.

All this already was enough for her to absorb in a day. And then he shocked her some more by telling her that he stayed near Gurgaon-Sohna Road and changed 2 buses everyday to reach the court or his office and it was a journey which comprised of atleast 2 hours each side. Once he reached the main road, he would stand near a flyover until his junior came to pick him up from there, and they either walked or took a cycle-rikshaw till the office.

After this *'normal routine journey'*, in his words, which for Sia amounted to a great ordeal, he would then begin his tasks with the same excitement every single day. Hearing this, Sia just felt a pain in her stomach. Her craving for an evening snack had vanished and she could not even finish the tea in her hand anymore.

What a brave man!!! Here she was, cribbing since morning about a simple auto journey in the heat from her home to the office that morning which had not even lasted more than 20minutes. Or crib about the fact that she had to walk a bit extra each day to find an autowallah or rikshawpuller to go to the nearest metro station. What was her effort and struggle compared to what this man was going through every single day??!

Sia could not believe he was so used to travelling every day from such a far off, area which could also expose him to some petty crimes and some unwanted elements trying to take disadvantage of his disability.

She was afraid to ask whether he had faced anything like this ever but next moment he himself told her that with time and experience he had developed a pretty good sense of direction. He could feel it when his destination would arrive and being an everyday task, he was pretty used to it by then. It was almost like a sixth sense which he had developed and little did Sia know then that she would get to see his sixth sense at full power in the days to come.

After this unique conversation, they had some discussions on the kind of work she would get to do. It seemed she was going to be pretty occupied in this one month and they discussed what his and her expectations from this internship were. Sia looked into those dark shades again. She felt a great sense of responsibility working under him. She felt like she had to prove herself to him. She had to be sincere and hard working and give her best. Sia knew he could not see her yet she kept wondering if she had enough formal clothes in her wardrobe for office. It was going to be an interesting one month for sure. They finally decided to call it a day and she left the office around 6p.m.

On the way back she took an auto again and kept recalling everything that had happened. But the memories of those two hours were engrained in her mind all the way home and for a long time. It was the strangest thing that had happened to her in her life till then. It was just the first meeting and she could make out that this man definitely had a sixth sense which worked wonders for him...

Wow Sia, so then what happened? You must have some incident worth sharing? He seems an interesting man I am sure you may have had some exciting stories to tell me ?, Siddharth was now too excited after hearing about the first meeting with Advocate Sameer Singh.

Sia looked at him and looked back at that wonderful month.

The Sixth Sense

It was true, that one month was and will remain the most memorable, unforgettable and learning experience of her life. Atleast so far, it had been. She was introduced to a new piece of legislation, got to know a lot about the problems faced by the persons who are differently abled (and not physically disabled) in the country in every walk of life, be it in jobs, public places, etc and got to meet and interact with a lot of them. Some were happy and content and the others she realized were extremely angry and the furious the way they were treated and discriminated against by people and the government the country.

Besides visiting courts with her sir and handling cases, Sia also did a lot of research on the law and read up various judgments of the high courts and the supreme court. As a part of her one month internship was to make a synopsis of as much as around 80-90 judgments and more if possible. It was one of those jobs wherein she was working for free yet at no point in time, did she feel like getting paid. Sia looked forward to each day at her new workplace buzzing with some new activity, some new event, some new case, issues, and would leave home as early as 8.30am to reach an almost empty office so that she could work in peace and concentrate on her work. Though there were many incidents which she could think of but at that moment she recalled one experience in particular which really made her realize about the Sixth Sense which she had observed in the first meeting itself.

There was an annual 2-day all India conference/meet on persons with disabilities from all over India, organized by the NGO itself alongwith some other similar organisations. Luckily Sia also got a chance to participate and attend the event being organized at an institute in West Delhi. There were eminent speakers, representatives of disabled communities from all over India and they being the organizers and the hosts, had to take care of everything from the arrangements to taking down notes of the speeches and so on. The conference was being held in the hall of one of the institutes there and the lunch was served in another adjacent building which was mainly a hostel.

Sia still remembered the incident very clearly. She and her sir reached the road leading upto the institute, in the morning and Sia escorted him to the building for the conference hall. However, as soon as they entered, he suddenly seemed hesitant to walk inside and stopped with a confused expression on his face. Sia looked at him and asked him what the problem was. To this he replied:

'Something is wrong Sia, I don't think this is the right place we have come to.'

A bit amazed at his comment, she looked around the reception area and it looked like it would have the conference hall inside. Plus she had also seen the institute's board outside so how was it possible that could she have been mistaken about the right building? Sia told him the same and yet, his confidence made her doubt her very action. Before she could say something more, her senior said this time with more confidence.

'No Sia, it just doesn't feel right. That place does not smell like it. I think this building is the hostel and not the main institute. Just see carefully there would be a board on your right with HOSTEL written on it.'

Anxious and fearing being proved wrong, Sia looked on her right only to get shocked all the more. There indeed was that very Board with HOSTEL written on it in bold letters and upon checking with the lady at the reception, it was indeed true that they were in the wrong building. The fact that it wasn't Sia who realized it but it was her senior was something weird and amazing at the same time. Sia was stunned beyond words and could not help resist an embarassed smile on her face seeing him smiling faintly at her.

Sia had heard that when a person's one sense is a bit weak, the others become stronger but this was her first experience and she was truly amazed beyond words at the confidence with which he knew he had come to the wrong place. With smiles on their faces, Sia and her mentor left the HOSTEL building and went to the adjacent building where in fact the event was taking place.

It was nothing less than magical for Sia….

Oh Wow Sia, this is really mind blowing! Why did you never share this incident with anyone not even me?" asked Sid while barging on his favourite Veg Hakka noodles and Veg Manchurian.

Sia did not know the answer to that question. Perhaps there are certain moments, experiences in a person's life which one never feels the need to share it with anyone. This was one of those rare experiences.

******

While Sia finished her story, she once again realized that no matter how many years had passed, it made Sia immensely proud that she once knew this man, that she got a chance to work under him and inspite of his unfortunate shortcoming, in that one month she could count on him and his judgment more than herself. And it was a feeling you don't get to experience with people in this world today; who have been gifted with everything by god and yet they do not value and cherish it. But Sameer Singh was gifted, and was truly special and unique in his own way. In that brief yet significant period, Sia realized that he was and is a wonderful man, to whom God had given an extraordinary will-power, determination, courage, an amazing, ever so-happy smiling nature, and a passion to make the most out of life with his strengths and weaknesses. Sia felt blessed, privileged and extremely proud of the fact that she got to spent one month of her life under the guidance of this unique man.

He was a man with a vision- and an extraordinary vision it was…

(Dedicated to Advocate Mr Pankaj Sinha, founder NGO PACE and Human Rights Activist whom the author had a privilege of working with in reality and who was supportive enough to have let me to write about him).

******

"The Confinement"

'Ut Poena Ad Paucos, Metus Ad Omnes, Perveniat'

That punishment may come to a few, the fear of it should affect all.

Part I

5. Jail No. 5

*J*ail- The word itself can send shivers down someone's spine and give him/her those goosebumps. It is, but of course, a place feared and dreaded by most normal and sane persons. We wish and hope that neither we nor our loved ones ever land up there, not even in our wildest of dreams. To add to our fears, a lot of Indian and Hollywood movies and TV shows including the then famous series *"Prison Break"* have shown the dark, gory, scary life of a prison along with the physical and mental torture it awaits a poor victim.

However, Sia had one unusual wish, something which she never revealed to anyone, for fear of being judged and mocked. The desire was an extra ordinary one, and it was to visit a prison one day (*hopefully for the right reasons*). She had waited and waited to get a chance but none of the previous NGOs also where she interned with earlier gave her an opportunity to visit any jail or prison to meet the undertrials or other prisoners.

Infact during her college days, one of Sia's favourite subjects was *Criminology*. A lot of people would not even have heard of this term. What was Criminology? It was basically the study of the mind and source behind becoming a criminal, how physical attributes also can sometimes differentiate a criminal from a non-criminal. How societal, family, and other factors affect the making of a criminal, the various theories on punishment, why and how juveniles ended up committing crimes, the history behind capital punishment, the case for and against it, the list was endless. All this and many more such interesting stuff made Sia glued to this subject more often than not and excited her more than a John Grisham novel.

As for the theories of punishment mentioned above, Sia also once read up that the reasons and motives behind punishing an offender could be manifold. It could be for the '*Deterrent effect*', i.e. the more harsher a punishment, the more it would prevent the crime from happening again. It would basically act as a deterrent for him/her and others to commit similar offence in the future. The deterrent theory however worked on the premise that an offender had done wrong and deserved to be punished for his wrong and unlawful deeds.

On the other hand, in stark contrast to the above was the '*Reformist theory*', a newly found concept. The supporters of this theory believed that the punishment could rather be for a much larger reformist purpose, i.e. to reform the criminal and bring him back to the society. This was based on the principle that no man was born a criminal from his mother's womb, it was the society and the circumstances that made him one. It is hence our duty not to penalize him, rather make him a better human being who is willing to live a better future and this is where prisons played a very important role.

In our country, unfortunately, focus was and still remains more on the deterrent effect and there were little/no steps to work towards looking at a criminal as a normal human being who also wanted to be happy and live a normal life. The deteriorating condition of the prisons, with not even the basic amenities and hygienic environment added to the ill health of the prisoners, often resulting in even deaths due to medical negligence.

The more Sia read and thought about this, the more she wanted to see a prison for herself to know its dark and ugly realities.

Even before Sia had pursued law, she had this deep end desire to visit a jail, more so because she had crossed one such prison several times everytime she would visit West

Delhi to meet her relatives. Specially on the eve of rakhi, the sight was worth capturing. There would be a long, a really long queue outside on the Jail Entry Gates which would stretch till more than a mile. And even when one had crossed that road, leaving behind the women, young girls and children waiting in the sun/rain to meet their brothers/fathers with a tired but excited look on their faces ,Sia would still keep looking back at them from her car window, until they were out of her sight. But the jail was never out of her mind.

Life in a prison was a different, rare, unique world in itself and Sia's life felt incomplete if she never got to get atleast a glimpse of it.

Sia was extremely curious to know and see for herself how really a prisoner lived. *What was the jail from inside and was it even a bit like how it was shown in the movies? What did they eat, how did they sleep, were they as dangerous as the crime they had committed? What did they do in the jail the whole day? What about the hundreds of those who had been wrongly arrested/convicted, what went on in their mind?* Were they getting any legal aid at all? All this and more kept cropping up in her mind all the time. People wanted to meet celebrities, all Sia wanted and wished for is to somehow get to meet a criminal.

And then as if God had heard her wishes, during her stint with an NGO in a city in India one fine day while she was working on drafting a writ petition, Sia got the shock of her life. She was told by one of the senior colleagues in the NGO that since they are currently working on a project on the state of prisons and undertrials in the country, hence on coming 27th August, they shall be visiting famous prison in the city to see the prison themselves and meet some of the undertrials as well.

"Oh ok mam" Sia replied. But only she knew what those words meant to her. Sia was stunned beyond words. *Had she lost her mind and senses or was she day dreaming? Was she hearing properly or there was something wrong with her ears?* Sia stood there, trying hard to hide her excitement even though she wanted to jump with joy and shout from the rooftops that her dream was finally going to come true.

Sia went home jubilant that day and told her family and friends like a kid got her favourite toy. Her parents found the whole idea somewhat twisted but knowing her, they already knew their daughter would go anywhow so they easily relented.

27th Aug 2012

Finally, the D-day arrived. It was a Monday. The said prison was one hour drive from their office since it was on the outskirts of the city. They were a group of 4 lawyers from the NGO, Sia being was among them and the timing fixed for their visit was in the afternoon, around 3pm. Considering the fact that they were going to a prison she felt an Indian attire would be best suited and Sia had been hand picked a white and blue salwar kameez for the important day bought by her mother.

They had to go inside Jail No. 5 and had almost walked

a mile from the parking that they were informed by one of the guards roaming nearby that they first had to go to the administrative department where they had to meet a certain official who would then take them to the concerned Jail. Tired in the sultry weather but not dejected, they turned around and started walking back towards the other end of the Jail entrance. It was only then that Sia started to see how vast the prison was, to how far it was spread. Finally, after a walk of another 15 minutes, they reached the gate from which Sia could see huge boards put up on the concerned block consisting of offices of all the Jail Superintendents and other officials. She went inside and was stunned at the sight.

'Gosh, is this green and plush or what??!!' was her first reaction as Sia stood there, mouth open, hands on her waist, trying to wonder whether she was really in a prison campus or had she mistakenly entered the JNU campus. *This JAIL, was, (and she is sure it still is), beautiful, literally, breath takingly, beautiful.*

Of what Sia could see and as far as she could see it was amazingly clean. From the spick and span smooth roads with huge trees on either sides, to the good looking and well maintained buildings which were in stark contrast to the otherwise government offices we detest. From the clean, healthy, pollution free air which she was not breathing even where she lived, to the neat and clean small gardens, everything was nothing less than a magical moment and a pleasing sight for all of them present there.

After some minutes of waiting, which was expected out of government offices, finally the man they had been waiting for came out of his room. He looked in his mid thirties, and was rather looking good in his bright uniform with several badges to compliment it. He finished the formalities and since there was an event going on in that particular jail, he arranged for two policemen to accompany them in the prison jeep which was parked outside the office.

Excited like small children, Sia waited with bated breath as they sat in the car and passed through the entire campus to reach the other end of the prison-and their final destination *Jail No 5* was written boldly on the board outside.

Ladies and Gentlemen, Boys and Girls, they had finally arrived……

Sia and the others got down from the car, feeling a bit privileged than when they had first entered the prison area. They were told to keep their bags and cellphones in the car itself and only to carry their wallets identity cards and case files. While they were doing the needful, Sia asked something which she should have known and assumed before but may be in all the commotion, it had skipped her mind totally;

'Sir, so what kind criminals are in Jail No 5?'

The policeman, for some reason *(which Sia understood after he finished)* looked at all of them but in particularly towards Sia, the only female among the group of 4 lawyers and said;

'It is the jail for all the male undertrials and convicts and between the age of 18-21 years.'

It did not matter to Sia. She knew she could handle male attention well. Filled with a new sense of determination and achievement, they started walking towards the entry gate. The huge, massive iron gate had a small opening on its left, a little low almost touching the ground, and it was just how they show in the movies! There was constant action and lots of men dressed in civil dress and policemen, were going in and coming out at a rapid pace. It definitely seemed like something large scale was happening inside, the function/event they had been told about was already going on and the noises reached even till outside.

One of the policemen then told them that for the entertainment of the prisoners, a laughter challenge programme had been organized in the Jail No. 5. Listening to what he had just said, they all started laughing. This was getting interesting every minute! Till now it was just a prison visit, and now they were also getting a bonus in the form of a live laughter challenge show!! The guard opened the small gate and went inside, followed by Sia and her team.

Once they entered inside, there was no sign of the jail yet. There was instead, yet another huge iron gate with a bigger lock on it which could have been more than her body weight. Now lay ahead the real sight, and Sia was beyond thrilled.

Finally, Sia was where she dreamt to be. She wished she could have captured that scene with a camera. It felt like absolutely a different world altogether. She never thought she would say this about a prison, but the first sight inside Jail No. 5 was splendid. It was vast; spread through acres, it was lush green, the layout was smartly thought of and designed. And well, Indian prisons were not that bad as projected after all. As they walked ahead, they then noticed that the sounds were coming from their right. And it was there that most of the people were moving towards.

By people, means there were lots of policemen, jail officials and yes, the offenders. They were casually strolling by and stood out among the crowd for the white attire they were in. While they walked towards and reached the park, where there were some performers on the stage and a large audience sitting as spectators, suddenly they heard another round of hootings, whistles and claps.

It didn't take Einstein to realize that this time it was not for the comedians but for the one girl Sia they had just seen! It was like rain had finally arrived in a drought-stricken area. Perhaps they might not be having frequent female visitors that too as young as her and perhaps as excited as Sia was. Her teammates were mocking her all the time. They then went nearer to the stage. Considering how hot and humid it was, they had put up tents and kept chairs on the side of the stage. The arrangement was pretty decent and impressive. They were made to sit on the right side of the stage and were supposed to actually watch the programme till it got over. *Of course they did not mind.*

As they settled down, Sia then looked around again to absorb where she really was. She was finally in the prison, luckily not as an offender, but as a lawyer, out there to meet an undertrial, , having a cup of tea, sitting in its lawn, watching a TV comedian (a sikh) crack jokes which had the prisoners in splits, and she had to accept that she was having a really weird, unpredictable but nice and fun time! After the famous sikh comedian was off the stage, it was time for the Special Guest of the day who was one of the leading stage comedians of that time and among those rare female comedians in the TV world. She was welcomed with more applause and a bunch of prisoners dancing in the lawn and she was an instant hit among them. She cracked jokes at herself, her being not so slim, the fact that she was in a prison, and even called some prisoners on stage and made them have a really good time.

They then watched a bunch of prisoners perform brilliantly, one sang a song, two of them did some acrobatics and few others danced to bollywood songs. These guys were really talented, Sia thought. But they had to do what they had come to do. And then the four of them, accompanied by the policemen and the official, finally set out to visit Jail No. 5 from inside.

Since they had come for the first time their NGO had arranged for a special visit to the jail premises before meeting the concerned undertrial for the case. They could see a small, open courtyard and just surrounding it were the prisons. They were then taken to one big room on the left which housed around 30-35 undertrials who all slept on the floor and there were many mattresses and bedsheets spread already. It had 3-4 fans which worked kind of decently.

Sia saw a small makeshift mandir (temple) made out in the wall at the extreme end of the room and few idols were kept there. She also saw many posters stuck on the walls of bollywood actors and actresses, which was again almost like they showed in the movies. There was a small bathroom at the left end of the room and curious about it too, she went and saw it from inside. So, there was one common bathroom for so many of them.

And well, it was dark, dingy and kind of spooky inside. One of the undertrials was standing with her and Sia did ask him few questions on how they lived here. *Was life manageable? Were the facilities ok?* He seemed pretty satisfied. He told her that there was a head count three times in the day, morning as soon as they got up, afternoon after lunch and later in the night. That they all lived like one big happy family in this huge room and barring one-two disturbing elements, lived in peace and brotherhood. He told that the food was ok and edible and they themselves mostly cooked it. Sia asked him about education and he did tell her that few ladies came in the morning (from those teaching campaigns perhaps) for teaching them English and Hindi but most of the guys here were hardly bothered. But, the interest was picking up gradually.

There were also a few already educated boys here and there was also a computer centre in the prison itself which was to be shown to us later. He told that the prison had started focusing a lot on extra activities to keep the prisoners occupied and develop their skills. There was also a placement programme in the nascent stages and he was very appreciative of the prison in a lot of respects. Talk about reformative punishment, Sia thought, this prison was taking steps in that direction for sure.

By then, Sia had developed a comfort level with this guy. *It was strange for Sia that the person giving her company was an undertrial, a criminal in this part of the world, someone about who she had no clue what crime he had committed. And yet somehow, it did not really matter anymore. He seemed a pretty normal guy at that moment to her and the supposed fear factor was non-existent in this prison experience.*

They came out of the room, and Sia looked around once again to absorb each and every aspect of it. She didn't know whether she would come here again, (*obviously not for the wrong reasons*), but nevertheless, all she wanted then was to click a complete mental picture of it in her mind.

They then crossed an interesting part of the prison, the place where few convicts (i.e. *to who punishment has been pronounced)* were kept. They were kept in isolation and did not have shared rooms. Also, there was the concept of *solitary confinement* which everyone had often heard of. Sia saw it in reality. The Jail official told them that whenever any of the prisoners got into a serious brawl, the person responsible would, as a punishment, be sent to one of these solitary confinement rooms. As the four of them stood there, Sia had a desire to go a bit ahead and see one of them if there was anyone inside. The man did mention that there may be 1-2 convicts present or sleeping. While Sia walked ahead, she was told to be careful and vigilant. Just next, she heard the official telling her;

'Beta, look closely in that room and that guy standing with the support of the grill. He has a small mirror in his right hand, and he uses it to find out and be alert and aware when someone is approaching him.'

As Sia went near his cell, they could actually clearly see the small mirror in his hand. For the first time, Sia had looked (*and a bit fearlessly*) in the eyes of a real criminal. Though, he did look scary, stone faced, well-built, and wasn't at all like the other undertrials they had met. He had this strange look on his face as if he was just staring right back at Sia with anger and restlessness. Sia observed him for a few seconds and after that looked in the other direction. Sia did not know for what offence he had been convicted for, but with that expression on his face, even if it was murder, she would not have been too surprised.

For the first time, the four of them spoke together and the same thing too;

'Sir, this is enough, let us get out of here and see the kitchen.'

Sia bit petrified by then walked out at a fast pace, much faster than how she had arrived to the cell, and now was headed towards the jail kitchen.

It was a huge hall again, and there was lots of commotion and noise. It was larger than a kitchen of a big fancy restaurant, after all food had to be prepared for hundreds of prisoners. The aroma of spices did awake their hunger pangs again. There were around 30-40 prisoners wearing aprons, toiling hard in the humid and hot to cook dinner. Some of them were sweating, but were engrossed in their tasks like efficient workers.

It was nothing less than a restaurant or hotel kitchen sight. And the way those boys were making round tandoori chapatis with ease and perfection, Sia looked at herself with guilt as even she could not get such shape and fluffiness when she tried to make during those rare times at home. There were also huge, large, round saucers and kadhais and they even saw the tons of daal and the mixed vegetables go into them. The food obviously did not look mouth watering or lip smacking and she wondered how the prisoners managed to eat it everyday.

But, compared to the image they already had in their minds, this was a stark contrast. It was really not how it she had expected it to be. For starters, the daal was not that watery as it was always projected it out to be! Sia was already in awe of the rotis and the prisoners could give the professional chefs a run for their money in this area totally. And she honestly felt with the effort they put in, the food would not be that bad after all. Even the kitchen was neat and clean and very well organized. The cooktops stretched till far and were spick and span. To their surprise, there was a special treat that day as a part of the function which was being held. They were making jalebis and pakoras for everyone including them, and Sia was looking forward to actually get to taste jail food for the first time in her life.

After much exploring which went on for longer than expected toppled with stares from the prisoners in the kitchen seeing a young girl meddling in their work, it was time to go and finally do what they had waited for long. It was time to bring into action our official purpose of visit- to meet the under trials and have a one-on-one discussion with them. The preceding events had generated enough curiosity in Sia to get to know them even more.

Things were finally turning out as she had planned. Infact, she had never anticipated such detailed exploration of the prison on her first visit from such close angles. And now was the time for the last event before the curtains would be drawn for the day.

It was going to be a like a face off; though just one of those of a criminal kind……..

******

(contd in part II ahead)

The Criminal

"Crimen Tahit Personam"

"The crime carries the person"

Part II: *(contd. from above)*

6. Qaidi No. 90. *(Prisoner No. 90)*

It was almost 5pm. The team had maximum one more hour with the prisoners, that is, if they were allowed to meet them till 6pm or they would have to take permission to come some other day. Their cell phones were in the car and Sia was worried of how many missed calls there had been from her home during the past 2-3 hours. But, she had to talk to atleast few of the under trials, know their stories, fill the forms given to her, and only then would their visit be worth while. The team was now taken to the computer room which was outside the jail cells, in a separate block outside a small garden. It was very close to where the stage had been put up earlier. By now, more and more under trials had arrived as the programme was almost nearing an end. Sia saw men and boys, dressed in white clothes, casual wear, few sikh prisoners, some strongly built hefty-looking men and few young college boys; there seemed an extremely unusual mix of people here.

Sia once again looked around the computer room, there was one particular under trial guy who was made the head of the computer department. He told us about all the facilities they had in the room. All the prisoners who had enrolled for the computer classes attended them few times in a week and were taught the basics of operating a computer; from either the fellow prisoners themselves or from external faculty. Sometimes, they were allowed to browse the internet too. He gave them some more information about the same as Sia listened to him attentively like she was back in her classroom and a young professor was addressing her.

The more Sia listened to that prisoner, the more she kept wondering what crime had he committed to land up here? He was certainly bit educated, spoke well in hindi and managed to speak few words of English, had a decent personality and seemed like a good organizer and leader. Everytime, he smiled at something, his face would light up and they would tinkle with the excitement of being the sole speaker even amidst a bunch of lawyers.

He seemed a bit mischievous as well as his smile always reached his eyes and they had a witty naughty expression. Finally, Sia and one of her colleague, who was probably having the same question in mind then asked him why was he was in the jail. *The words he uttered next sent a shiver down their spine.* With the same tone and bluntness, he answered their question without even pausing for a minute or batting an eyelid. *He looked them in the eye and told that he was in jail and was accused of raping a girl.* There. Straight out, in the open. He said it out loud and clear and in their faces.

For a few seconds they were all quiet, trying to absorb what he had just said. And then he continued. He told them that the girl was his girl friend and his version of the story was that the girl's family had wrongly framed him for the offence of rape. *That was perhaps his side of the story.* Ofcourse he could have been bluffing. Or may be he could have been right. No one knew. No one could guess either. Sia wanted to believe he was speaking the truth. He was certainly a smooth talker she thought. He had been in the Jail for quite a few months now and though some lawyer had taken up his case, yet he had accepted his life here easily. He seemed even comfortable and satisfied in his small world in Jail No. 5.

Having absolutely nothing to respond to what he had just told them and the way he had said it, Sia decided to move on. She went inside and among the four of them, it was going to be 1-2 under trials each. As they did not have much time, they could not interview all of them. There were around 40 prisoners inside and outside the room by then and though they would have loved to talk to all of them, yet time did not permit them to do so. Sia remembered vividly till date the man she interviewed and his story and his face is still etched in her mind clearly.

He was Qaidi No. 90 /Prisoner No. 90. Atleast that's what she was supposed to know him as since his name was not to be revealed. He must have been in his late twenties. He had a medium built, short height for a man and had rough messy black hair, with few strands falling onto his forehead. He wore a cream/white coloured shirt with a check design with a darker shade of trousers/pants. His shirt was half tucked in a loose way and he had a cute smile on his face throughout. He sat opposite to Sia on a table while she sat on a chair, with the form in one hand and a pen in her other hand with no idea what kind of a weird interview this was going to be.

At first Sia was a bit shy. A girl with so many words who was never scared of initiating a talk anywhere, words were failing here. After a long long time, she was hesitant and nervous did not know how to start, what to say. He seemed willing to chat but was waiting for the green signal and first step from the girl in front of him. Sia finally mustered up the courage and broke the ice. They started talking about him. She told him she wanted to know his story and what had he done to land up here. She just listened as he told began by telling her that he belonged in a small colony in a remote part of the city.

He had dropped out of school at a tender age due to

family constraints and was doing some part time jobs to make ends meet. He had a younger sister and while talking about her, his expression became gloomy. Sia could feel that his being here was perhaps related to his sibling and all sorts of random negative thoughts cropped up in her mind. And then he revealed the story, or his side of it.

One unfortunate day, some roadside boys teased her while she was on her way near the house. He knew the guys who were involved in it. As he got to know about it, an altercation took place between him and one particular guy. And as normally happens, in a fit of rage and anger, he took out a knife and stabbed him. He told Sia that he used to carry the knife around with him just to show off and for kicks, he confessed with a tinge of a smile. *That he did not feel wrong in carrying it, was clearly evident.* The guy was injured and upon witnessing it and perhaps out of fear, this under trial ran off with his friends. In haste, he threw the knife somewhere in a nearby drain. Few hours passed and he returned back home.

He knew things had gone out of hand but he was confident he would not be caught. But as luck would have it, the police caught hold of the knife which led to his arrest and put him under custody. A case was established against him and he was then put in this prison. And it was someone known and close to him who had been the informer to the police, he told in a grim tone.

Sia heard out his story attentively her mind was brimming with curiosity.

'Toh bhaiyya ji, aapko gussa agaya aur aapne chaku maar dia?', Sia asked with a puzzled look on her face.

(So, brother, you got angry and in a fit of rage you stabbed him?)

'Madam, bas meri behen ko chheda usne, mujhe gussa agaya. Maine chaku nikala, aur maar dia use'. He retorted.

(Madam, he teased my sister, I could not bear it, I took out the knife and hit him.)

'Aur pata nahi madam kaise police ko chaku mil gaya humne toh faink dia tha'. Shayad mera hi koi dost ya jankaar tha jisne dhokha de dia". He confessed rather sheepishly.

(I have no clue how the police got hold of that knife. Maybe my own friend stabbed me in the back and informed about me.)

"Par aapne chaaku kyun maara, ye gunaah hai apko pata hoga na"? Sia wanted to know each trivial detail of this case now.

(But why did you stab him, you knew this is an offence right?"

'Madam behen ka sawaal tha, hum kya karte, us samay jawaan the, garam khoon tha, bas hogai na galti madam ji', he immediately retorted this time rather firmly.

(Madam, it was the question of my sister's honour. I was young short tempered, it all just happened.)

He narrated all this (and more) to Sia all this with a straight, calm, composed face smiling all the time. He knew he had done wrong but somewhere he was proud of the fact that he took a stand for his own sister howsoever even thought he had taken the law in his hands. His act was punishable howsoever justifiable it may have been. And then the conversation went further;

'Aap akele hi hain ya shadi shuda, koi biwi?? (Are you married or single?)' Sia tried to divert the conversation suddenly no more keen on knowing the details of the incident anymore

'Madam ab toh yahan 4-5 saal hogaye, beech mein bail bhi mili, bahar gayaa, behen ki shadi kara di. Meri bhi zindagi me ek ladki thi, jab dubara bail mili toh maine bhi shadi karli usse.'

(Madam, I have been here for 4-5 years, and in between I was even out on bail. I got my sis married in the meantime and also married the love of my life.)

And he smiled again, this time a wider grin on his face. To this, even Sia could not help but smile but she was tad surprised too;

'Shadi? Toh ladki ke maa baap shadi ke liye maan gaye? Unhe toh pata hoga na aap jail me ho?'

(Married? And what about the girl's parents, how did they agree?)

'Toh aur kya madam ji, sab pata tha, par ladki ne zid kar li. Pyaar karte the, karli shadi, kabhi kabhi ajati hai milne yahan parr. Yaad to aati hai par ek din toh yahan se zarur nikal jaunga na. He was quick to answer:

He continued;

"Par madam, yahan to mere jaise bahut hain, aur kai toh aise hain jinka koi apraadh hai bhi nahi, bas unhe pakad ke jail

mein daal dia hai. Kismet ke maare bechare. Kabhi koi vakeel ajata hai kabhi koi nahi, filhal mera case ek nayi vakeel sambhal rahi hai, kuch dinon me agli taareekh hai"…he paused then stated in a grim tone, *shayad kuch acha ho jaye is baar.*'

(Yes they knew everything about me, but we were in love and the girl took a stand. She sometimes visits me here. Ofcourse I miss her but one day I will be free from here. But there are many her like me, stuck for years. And many are even innocent, just victims of destiny. Sometimes lawyers come for our help, sometimes no one does. My case is being handled by a female lawyer now and I have a hearing scheduled in the next few days. Maybe something positive comes up.)

Sia had been listening to his story with utmost interest and concern. He seemed like a happy go lucky guy who was simply at the wrong place at the wrong time. So many accidents go unnoticed, so many go scot free. And yet, there are so many undertrials here in this prison and many more who have been spending months and years rotting in the jail for sometimes petty crimes and sometimes as mere suspects for no fault of their own, Sia wondered. It was heartening to know this and the fact that sometimes they did not even know why they were arrested at the first place and when they would be set free. They had no idea what was the law, under which provision were they punished, what was the remedy available to them and yet, their faces projected an optimistic and content attitude. That may be, they had accepted their present life as their destiny and moved on, that they were still hopeful that one day they would come out of here and go into the real world.

Thinking all this and looking at her undertrial, Sia eyes had turned moist, but that was not the place to cry and she probably had to save them for later. She secretly wiped her face with her dupatta and filled in the details in the form, ofcourse omitting the ones she was not supposed to have known at the first place.

After chatting with him and some others for few more minutes, it was time for the team to conclude the chit chats and gear up for the final goodbyes and leave. It was now 5.45pm and they were already getting late.

The reformist theory Sia had studied came into her mind then again. Sure, the prison had changed, it was keeping the prisoners occupied but perhaps the ideal way was to not keep guys like them in the prison at the first place. May be make them do something for the society, some social service, maybe serve the very family whose member they had injured, get a chance to redeem themselves. And atleast use their potential for some constructive use than wasting each day in the prison doing nothing at all. But such was the law of the land and of God and one had to pay for his sins in this form itself, in this life itself.

The eventful day was finally nearing its end and what better way to end it than by having and savouring the hot and yummy looking pakoras and jalebis made from the hands of the very prisoners teamed up with hot nice tea. Even they enjoyed serving theteam and kept forcing them to eat more and more. Pakoras, jalebis, and tea. It was a perfect threesome combination Sia thought.

As the team of budding lawyers stood there eating them, it was six in the evening and the sun had almost set. It had begun to get dark. And it was time to finally go.

The team said their goodbyes, thanked the officials for their support, thanked the prisoners specially the computer room head and walked towards the same gate, the small opening of *Jail No. 5*, exiting towards the main road. The long day had finally come to an end. Those three hours from 3pm to 6pm seemed like an entire lifetime, atleast to Sia. Sia went home and shared the entire day's drama like a thriller movie being unfolded scene by scene with her family. And then, she shared it on the phone with few of her friends. And then again ,it continued the next day in her office. Sia often thought about it for the next few days and even felt that the real litigation and the real purpose of becoming an advocate was to infact help such prisoners and undertrials.

But then, like the rest, ambition got the better of her and she got busy and entangled in the web called LIFE and moved on with her future assignments. But, the impact of the entire prison episode must have certainly been too deep. Because even years after the incident, everytime Sia thought about this day, each and every image of whatever part of the prison she had seen, of whatever she heard inside, whatever she saw and spoke and experienced came back to her with amazing clarity. And most of all, she could never forget Qaidi No. 90

******

EPILOGUE:

LOOKING BACK: Life as a Law Student

This one is dedicated to all my friends at my law college, most of whom I am not in touch with, yet I want them to know that I think about them everyday…well ok that is an exaggeration, not everyday but definitely more often that they might have expected. I can never forget the 'famous' Campus Law Centre, my law college, the place where I spent three critical years of my life which eventually altered the course of my life and brought me where I am today.

Years later, one fine day, while I was crossing the University area with my friend as he had some work in the administrative department, I could not resist myself from paying a short visit to the place which was my abode for three long years. As I reached the college gate and walked inside, a strong sense of nostalgia hit me hard.

I had spent those 3 whole long years reaching the "sought after" North Campus, changing all sorts of modes of transport possible- from bus to auto to metro to rikshaw to car to walking. You name it, and I had used it. It used to be a mission reaching the college and the cherry on top was being told sometimes that the concerned teachers had not turned up, or more often than not we were just sitting outside and not entering the class without any reason whatsoever.

As I walked in, it was as if my feet routinely took me to my favourite bench from where I could get the best view. I looked around the entire campus and memories of each place started to flood my mind. It was the same big banyan tree, the same guy selling the hot favourite bantas(lemon sodas) where the guys had their endless chai sessions as well. All the latest gossip revolved around this banyan tree and it was home to diverse discussions every single day. I could not resist the urge to walk upto the small Nescafe Kiosk, and my eyes fell upon the sitting area where after each class, our (in) famously loud girl gang of around 7-8 laughed like crazy on literally anything under the sun. a lot of pictures had been clicked near this Nescafe area and as I recalled a faint smile passed my lips and I ordered my staple cold coffee and chocolate muffin which still tasted exactly the same.

Just as I sat on a bench to savour my coffee, I saw few girls giving packets of milk and biscuits to a bunch of cute puppies and I recalled how this was the first sight we used to see when we would reach the college around 8.30am in the morning. As usual I could not muster up the courage to hold a puppy despite how cute and adorable he or she was and I enjoyed the sight from a distance as always.

This college made me witness student politics at its best and *worst, particularly during the university election time in August-September each year. The constant hooting, demonstrations, random altercations, chanting of slogans disrupted classroom schedules and I could not help but remember how it actually made us all excited and pumped up to visit the college despite being told by our parents to stay at home during those times.*

*As I saw the huge rush at the book seller at one corner near the banyan tree, it brought a much wider grin on my face. I had experienced the concept of Semester exams for the first time while pursuing my law degree and boy was it an ordeal. It always felt like we were simply giving exams after exams. Those three hour exams simply seemed like a never ending phenomenon. While we were just beginning to breathe a sigh of relief as one term ended, another one would commence soon thereafter and "study mode" was on at the blink of an eyelid. While being a high achiever all my life, this college made me realized for the first time the value, the real value and worth of getting a damn 60. Getting more than 60% was a huge, really a big deal in my college and maintaining it was a bigger challenge. To everyone's surprise (I am sure), I had been a part of the "**60 special**" league from the first term itself and looking back I realize how crazily tough it was to get above 60 in each term.*

*As I saw few students clad in black and white attire in the campus, it did not take much time to fathom that it was not the new college dress code but it was something else. I assumed they were most probably pursuing their "Internship". I recalled this word at an instant. In this place and I am sure in similar law colleges, "**Internships**" were and still would be THE in-thing. Coming to college in black and white meant that you* were interning under a lawyer or in a law firm or somewhere similar. The moment one would enter, the first question asked to you would be **"where are you interning**??!!

It would surprise me when random batchmates would ask me this perennial question but with time I got used to it. One would be the talk of the town incase he/she had landed an internship in some reputed law firm or under a famous lawyer. Thinking of internships, it evoked in me the thought how to my utter surprise, law taught me that money had to be sidelined many a times and the notions of **"won't work unless paid"** had to be sidelines more often than not.

But those were some fun times.

It had been almost one hour since I had been inside the campus and fearing glances from students around me, I decided it was time to say goodbye. As I walked out and went ahead towards Patel Chest, the sight of few buses excited me like a small kid. It reminded me of my most wonderful memory me, the reason law school was and remained extremely special- **THE U-SPECIAL**. Thanks to my three year stint with law, I discovered a novel university special bus which was an amazing and wonderful experience. Not to forget my bus gang , a crazy gang which laughed out loud and chatted and argued like hell. Travelling in the U-special was the biggest motivation which made me wake up at 5.45am in the morning to reach the bus stop by 7.45am. Never ever did I feel that going to college early in the morning would be so much fun and the long distance would be covered in no span of time. More than anything, I missed the U-special and my gang badly and the moment I saw it I forced my friend to catch the one which would drop me near my office.

I wished I could go back in time, I wished I was not an employee but a student again. It hit me that I had an office to report to and with moist eyes, I said goodbye to my college. I bid adieu to the road which led to my college, the North Campus with all of its hustle bustle hoping to return one fine day for a much longer period of time. The same buildings, the same line of trees, the same aloo chat and bhelpuri wallah, the same bus stand where I spent hours waiting for the U-special, everything seemed the same, yet everything had changed. **For, change was and is the only constant in life.** *And well yes, this crazy 'Life' had to move on. And it had moved on indeed. I again wished I could be here again.*

For, I truly and earnestly believe, there is no wonderful phase in a person's life, than living the life of a student.

******

ACKNOWLEDGEMENTS

This book is in a way a small attempt to give back something in return to my family (Mom, Dad & MeghAdi) and my extended family and loved ones for all the love and affection they have been constantly bestowing upon me always.

I would also like to extend my sincere thanks to Leadstart Publishing and Wordit Art Fund for enabling me to get this book published, for actually responding to my 6 year old email and give me an opportunity to finally see my name on a book cover. Heartfelt thanks to Ms Pooja and Ms Miral for their constant help and support, their valuable inputs, ideas and guidance in making my dream come true.

I cannot end this book without thanking publicly (*for the first time*), my life partner and my best friend since time immemorial, my husband *Sulabh Saini*. He is the sole reason I am what I am and where I am today. This book would not have been possible if not for his constant support, motivation and if he had not taken the pains to read, review and give suggestions to make this book turn out this way. For someone who is diametrically in contrast to me when it comes to the habit of reading, I thank him whole heartedly for making the extra effort to read and discuss the stories with me till late nights after his long arduous days (*thanks to GST*). Not to forget that those chats were coupled with the endless baby diaper changing, feeding, crying and napping sessions.

Thank you for keeping up with my tantrums, mood swings and my twitchy nature while this book was at its last stages. The months leading up to the publishing of this book have been one of the most fun filled, exciting and memorable days of my life. Thank you for suggesting the wonderful book cover and helping me design it the way I had imagined to make the book look the way it is. And finally, thank you for being there for me, forever and always.

******